THE LION OF THE UNDERWORLD

KEVIN HARRIS

Copyright © 2022 by Kevin Harris

Paperback: 978-1-958381-60-1
eBook: 978-1-958381-61-8
Library of Congress Control Number: 2022917884

All rights reserved. No part of this publication may be reproduced, stored in a retrieval system, or transmitted by any means, except for brief quotations in printed reviews, without the prior permission of the publisher, Pam Vause.

This is a work of nonfiction.

SWEETSPIRE LITERATURE
—— MANAGEMENT ——

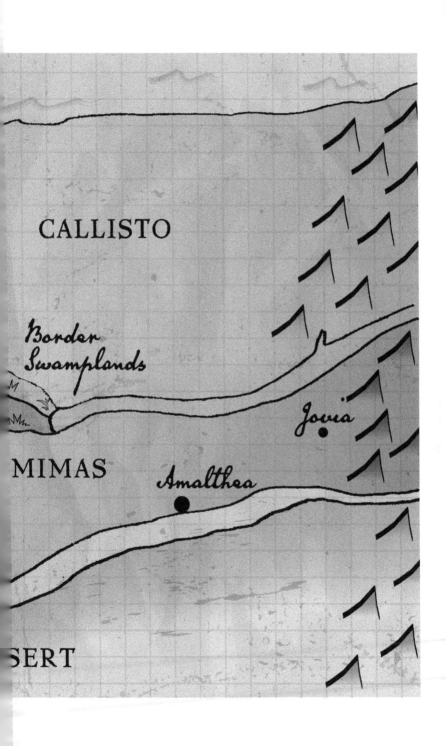

TABLE OF CONTENTS

CHAPTER ONE

THE WATCHFUL

The spring sun shone gently as Lieutenant Kingswood rode slowly into the City of Almathea.

Flanked either side by towering stone walls, the high wooden double gates were swung back so the many traders could pass freely. Kingswood could not ever remember seeing it so busy. Some travelling in caravans, some on foot leading their laden donkeys behind them.

It was great to see, thought Kingswood, "But if one trader more bumps into my mount; I will run him through with my sword!. After all, I am an officer now. I can do whatever I want I please" he laughed out heartily "Uh, I was only jesting" he explained quickly to a formidable looking old woman who stopped to scowl at him. "Lieutenant Kingswood?" enquired a young faced soldier standing in his way. A curt nod answered him. "Captain Nicolus asked me to meet you and see to your mount".

"The man never loses a moment" sighed the officer wearily. Kingswood was still a young man himself, certainly the youngest man to hold such a rank in Minmas. His light brown hair flopping untidily in the breeze made him look even younger still. "He is in his chambers?". A polite "yes sir" led him to dismount. Though slim, he loomed over the short soldier and inspected his clean and well kept uniform.

"Thank you soldier, try not to dirty those pretty garments of yours" he added with an impish smile.

A short while later he was walking briskly along a cold stone passage. "This place is like a bloody rabbit warren!" He exclaimed out loud as he came to a shiny light oak door. He knocked hard twice and entered sharply as a soft voice beckoned him in.

The chamber was quite large with a high vaulted ceiling. The wide leaded windows gave plenty of daylight. Standing in front one of the windows, looking out was a grey-haired distinguished looking officer. "Sit down Lieutenant". The man still spoke softly and smiled pleasantly as he turned around. "Lieutenant" he repeated," it sounds just !." As does Captain, Sir" replied Kingswood with a big childish grin.

"Indeed", saving the wealthy trading quarter of Amalthea, does help to court friends". Both men chuckled but the Captain stayed standing behind his new walnut desk, the much older man now looked solemn. "Though only this Winter past, that attack by the Maraunders, could have brought Mimas to her knees" he said with disgust. "Without our wealth we could not afford our armies" agreed Kingswood thoughtfully. "The threat is still there" warned the older man as he turned round to look out the window once more. "That raiding party had trained men, cannons and barges to ferry them. A great deal of riches were required to mount that devious venture".

"You suspect other lands behind the attack, Sir?". You told the Council you could not be sure. It could even have been some prosperous merchants from Callisto, I remember you saying".

"You are wise beyond your years, Kingswood. That is why I picked you from the ranks, not for your sword hand". Captain Nicolus still did not look from the window.

The young officer knew he sought praise too hard from his Commander, like a hound with his master. "Everyone knows that Callisto longs for our furtile pastures but Charon would do anything to make their ancient City Deimos, great once more. Years of fighting the Sea Raider fleets have taken their toll but their soldiers are bred for conquest."

"You are right Lieutenant, you are right" remarked the older man in a tired voice as he stepped away from the window. "We must move, - wisely. If we run around barking like a guard dog to everyone we mistrust, we will be in the biggest war these lands have ever seen. One we are not yet ready for". The grey haired man realised he had become too grave and took a deep breath to calm himself.

"The High Commander of Mimas relies on my information to protect this land". The Captains voice was now quiet and measured. As you know he can only steer the Council of Almanthea. The Council is full of scared men at this time. Scared of war, scared of losing what they hold dear. Knowledge is power, Lieutenant and we need to keep that knowledge flowing to the Council. So they can make the right choices!."

Captain Nicolus sat down heavily in his chair, his face looked worn. "I have chosen you to be tasked to the Principality of Diore on our South West border. You know most of our trade come through there. For over two score years the merchant caravans have travelled from distant lands untouched through the Io Desert to Diore. Five days ago a caravan was razed to ashes. Two days ago Io Tribesman attacked a sail barge from Diore with flaming arrows. I need to know what is happening down there and why!. We have forgotten our allies, Lieutenant, the two of you will be there for a long time, watching, learning and building trust"."It would be an honour Sir" said Kingswood beaming with pride. "Sir, - you said the two of you?".

\#

Breathing heavily, sweat dripped down his bare chest. Every sinew strained as Ben's two swords carved through the air. He knew to practice in open land was unwise. To practice in the unfriendly lands of Callisto in daylight was clearly foolish. Ben Hawks was not a complete fool though. He had been watching movements of farmers, travellers and soldiers here for a while now. Knowing he was heading back to Mimas this morning, there was a matter he was eager to put to rest beforehand.

Ben loved to practice his newly acquired skills and was confident there was no army patrols around for the time being. He had hoped that somebody else would come across his path before he returned.

"What have we here?" enquired a gruff voice. Ben turned his head to see two men on mounts and another driving a horse and cart. The cart had made such a din he was not startled by these strangers.

"He has some nice battle scars, but is not one of our soldiers with those black trousers" cried one of the mounted men. "He looks more like us, a hunter" said the man sitting on the cart.

Ben stood upright right, revealing his tall, taunt stature. He looked up to see this man had a big metal cage on the back of his cart. Uttering deep rumbling growls inside was the unmistakable brown bulk of a bear inside. "Oh, - I am nothing like you" he snarled as his dark brown eyes shone defiantly. "I have been watching you three for a while. Stealing kills off honest hunters. Smuggling rotten meat over the border, causing sickness and disease. He glanced up at the cage again and his anger grew. "To wrench a magnificent beast from the wild to perform tricks in a dirty town?. It will not happen!" , his voice was thick with determination as his grip tightened on the hilts of the swords.

"Is that so?" replied the man with the gruff voice on the other mount with a nasty grin. The man was tall like Ben but more burly. His face was scarred and unwashed, his short black hair was greasy and unkempt. He waved the other horseman forward and the rider pointed his long barrelled musket at Ben's chest. "With your brown eyes and hair, you could be from Callisto" remarked the thug who Ben now understood to be the head man. "I do not think so. Now, we will take your weapons and your brute of a mount over there. Then after beating you senseless, we will sell your hide to our soldiers" he laughed cruelly.

Fear was drifting through Ben's body but he did not want to show these cut throats that. "Will I be locked in a cage staring out at three stinking, dumb animals?" he enquired thoughtfully with a thin smile.

The men burst out with laughter as they grinned at each other. "It is only one bear, you stupid oaf!"cried the head man, still laughing.

"I was talking to the bear". The laughter stopped abruptly and the headman hissed through his broken black teeth. "I want his swords now!!!".

"Careful what you ask for" whispered Ben, his eyes still on the headman. He stepped forward and as he span around, a sword flew from his leading hand. The man with the musket screamed loudly as the straight bladed weapon speared his right shoulder. The musket went off as he dropped to the ground. The shot harmlessly raked the earth as Ben did a forward roll towards the cart. Rising to his feet he threw his second sword with all his might. The dull curved blade clattered the cart driver's legs. Shocked, the man dropped the musket he was fumbling with and fell backwards. With a bellowing roar the driver then abruptly flew through the air and landed face first into the grass. The enraged bear had taken exception to his presence.

"Should have stuck both men in the chest, must work on that!". Ben kept his eyes on his quarry, he could see the panic in the headman eyes as he realised he was now alone." If your friends live, then so be it. Alas, you - " he carried on and his voice become more dangerous.

"You,- are responsible for these crimes and will come with me to face judgement".

The headman was now looking to flee until his eyes flickered evilly. "You had me for a moment stranger" he laughed nervously. "You have no more swords and I have my flintlock pistol ready to fire". He patted his weapon resting in his shoulder strap.

Ben's eyes narrowed on the man, still in his saddle. "This not a game of luck you play in a Tavern!" he warned in despair.

The headman gave a sneer of defiance. "Yet, I chance!, you will not get to your swords in time! he spat and snatched at his pistol.

In one swift motion Ben dropped to his knees and slipped a short knife from his boot. As he lunged forward the blade thudded into the chest of his foe. The headman groaned in disbelief, his body contorted in pain as his pistol slipped from his fingers. He tried to speak but no words came out as he slumped forward on his mount.

"You were right, I did not get to my swords in time" he said quietly shaking his head in disbelief. "YOU LOT ARE DUMBER THAN SHEEP! He cried loudly. "DO I LOOK LIKE A JESTER?. WAS THIS MERRIMENT FOR YOU?? He shouted in an exasperated tone. He cursed loudly at the heavens as the bear roared, snapping him from his thoughts.

"You are right, my friend, we all need to leave here swiftly". The cart driver was still face down in the grass, moaning pitifully, as Ben searched his pockets for the key to the locked cage. Moments later, he threw the heavy padlock away and strode purposely over to the man he had impaled with his sword.

"Hurting or not, if I was you, I would drag your friend to your mount and ride like the wind".

"Or what?, you will slay us as well?" hissed the man through his clenched teeth. Ben freed his sword with a sharp tug, smiling as he did so, "not me", Her!", he nodded to the cage whose metal door had began to creak open.

Holding his shoulder, the wounded man frantically got to his feet, hobbled over to his friend and painfully pulled him up. Ben watched laughing as the pair rode away, cursing wildly as they clung to the galloping mount.

He turned to the big beast as it lumbered from the cage. It rose up on it's hind legs and sniffed at the air. Staring right at him the bear gave a bellowing roar, then tugged down the remains of a deer from the side of the cart. Like a contented dog with a bone clamped in her jaws, she ran for the nearest trees.

Feeling fairly contented and pleased himself, he removed the harness from the cart horse and led it to the head man's mount. He pushed the body crashing to the ground and searched his garments. "We keep what we gather" he murmoured. Finding a purse of coins he led both horses to his own mount. Titan, a wheat shaded draught horse was now calm after the drama and got back to his favourite pastime, eating grass!. Ridiculed by his fellow guardsman on his choice of mount, he could not wish for a stronger, more sure footed beast for the perilous mountains he used to patrol. "Time to leave" he ordered himself. He knew he had acted dumbly this morning out of anger. His eyes then fell on the wooden cart with the offending cage. "Very well, the very last dumb act for today!".

# #

Later that morning, he crossed over the border into Northern Mimas with no one in sight. Hot and weary, Ben, Titan and their spoils of victory made their way to a small nearby farm. The Guardsman waved enthusiastically, as a short, bald headed man, bent over with age, came over to greet him.

"Tom, good to see you" he cried cheerfully. "You can tell your sons and their families, there will be no more rotten meat coming over the border for a while!".

The old man looked uncomfortable and peeked over his shoulder. "That will bring joy to many folk here, young Ben. "We thank you from the bottom of our hearts, but - , we - expected you sooner". Ben's broad shoulders slumped and he gave a small sigh". "I know Tom but I wanted to end it before I, you said we, Tom?."

"If Captain Nicolus heard of this, you would end your days cleaning out the barrack stables in Jovia!!. The firm voice came from the open doorway of the farmhouse and Ben groaned as he saw Lieutenant Kingswood striding towards him. "IF, the Council heard of this, you would end your days at the gallows. Which, shortly after, I would be a sergeant stuck in this fly – infested patch of mud!.

"No offence Tom" he added sincerely to the old farmer.

"Think nothing of it, Lieutenant Kingswood, I never liked it here". The officer turned to face the man with a befuddled look. He opened his mouth to say something, then shook his head and looked back at his Sergeant. "Tom, could you water this excuse of a mount" he asked politely, still staring at the guardsman. "Take the other two beasts afterwards, they are now yours." Sergeant Hawks, dismount and present your report".

Ben wrenched a parcel of parchment from his backpack and handed them swiftly over, Kingswood sat on the grass, cross-legged and started reading. "Your strict instructions were to observe the Callisto side of the border and not to engage anyone. He spoke coldly without looking from the parchment. "What is that smoke I can still see from the direction you came from?". Ben nervously explained about the fight but left out that he had laid in waiting for the men.

"So you vanquished three drunken thugs and a cage?, well then, I can tell Captain Nicolus that all our problems have been solved!!". "Pray tell, what would happen if I had to order you right back there to gather some pivotal information for Mimas?". In an land where every musket carrying soldier of Callisto is now looking to kill something?".

"I would be dead by dawn" mumbled Ben, staring at the ground. He greatly respected Kingswood and first met him when he was a Great Sergeant. He knew he would still be bored and restless in his home town of Jovia, were it not for him.

The Lieutenant was still reading, his sharp eyes flickered with interest. "Yes, you would be very dead by dawn". "Worse still, thousands of lives could suffer because Minas did not have the full picture off what is happening on her own border!". "We - all must move and think more wisely, or the consequences will be dire for everyone". "Hmmm, this is good work Sergeant". "You say Sister Anne taught you to read and write?, they should make her a Saint!!". Now the Lieutenant looked up, wearing his usual broad smile. "Tell me, have you ever been to the Principality of Diore?".

#

The heavy curved swords clashed loudly as the two bare chest warriors attacked each other without mercy. The smaller but more youthful man danced around his great opponent, his face a mask of determination, never standing still long enough to greet one of the many vicious blows aimed at his body. He had fought like this before, his swiftness was unnatural, then he would deliver the fatal blow in front of the cheering crowd that watched the contest in the circle of stones. Alas this man would not tire, the huge shaven head warrior charged at him like an unrelenting bull, blow after blow rained down on him. When he tried his own crippling attack, his opponent was just out of reach or barely managed to parry his blade, always he was close, so close but so is the fox who tries to outwit the Cobra, he thought.

Against this warrior, a monstrous beast with a skilful hand, he knew his spirit, courage and skill had to as good as he imagined in his dreams. His strength was leaving him and now his chance was fading.

With a cry of defiance spurred on by the baying crowd he sprang to meet his opponents strange sword, adorn with runes etched into the curved blade, gleaming in the burning sunshine. As it fell down at his head, he side stepped and raised his longer, sleeker blade high at an angle, deflecting the brutal blow harmlessly into the flat barren ground with his own, trapping it there. Struggling desperately against the raw strength of his opponent, he tried to step on the man's shaking sword, but was a moment too late. A gigantic brown elbow flew up onto his chin, his head rocked back violently as he stumbled away. Only a true courageous warrior like himself could stay standing now as the crowd span around, as if caught in a giant whirlwind. He bravely clenched his teeth and stamped his foot down hard to clear his mind but as he looked up he could only see that same gleaming blade scythe towards his throat.

The victor raised his bloodied sword to the chanting crowd, breathing heavily, he bowed respectfully to the body of the slain fighter. Gathering his breath he slowly walked over to the edge of the circle and barked a loud laugh as he stood in front of three pale looking men. "I trust you liked my little display ?", he asked looking very pleased with himself. It was clear the younger man of the three was ready to be sick. He and the man standing tall and proud next to him wore dark grey uniforms. The tall man was cleanly shaven and his clean black hair was cut short. A long sheathed sabre hung from his belt on the left and he rubbed his chin in thought. He slowly nodded his head in begrudged approval. "You are indeed very strong, and – good with the sword".

"I think, what Lieutenant Otto means, is that your swordmanship is legendary in Charon and we are honoured to witness such a contest, Murquin the Overpowerer". This man was much shorter than the others and his small black beard made him look smaller still. Unlike the others he wore a plain white tunic with a gold coloured collar and baggy brown trousers. He was not standing tall and proud but looked confident and wise. "Indeed, a most satisfactory show from a tribal chief of such renown". "We have chosen the right ally" he added happily.

The large warrior was still looking at Lieutenant Otto with a knowing expression as he gestured with the open palm of his hand. "Please – this way, our talk is not for the ears of others". He led the men away from the crowd to a group of brightly coloured tents. Apart from a figure dressed from head to toe in a plain white cloak following behind them, they were now alone.

The tribal chief nodded to the gangly figure who walked briskly over, wrapped a white flowing cloak over the chiefs wide and muscular torso, bowed and stepped back once more. The robe seemed to make the chief even more imposing, his blue eyes looked on with great zeal.

"Charon has chosen me because I am the only man with the vision to do what must be done. The caravan and barge were merely the beginning. After my next attack, Diore will be forced to act and show their true face," he remarked evenly. No more trade will come through the desert for Mimas and Diore, only Charon".

"We have the first chest of gold as agreed" said the bearded man eagerly as he waved the young man forward carrying a heavy looking backpack.

"Good Leon, my desires are pure but alas, greed is useful to help create this vision". The gangly tall figure gently removed the backpack as if it was empty.

Leon cleared his throat and carried on. "Can we supply anything else?, muskets?, gunpowder?, I myself have invented some of the latest killing instruments" he boasted smugly.

"I have everything I require" replied Murquin in a deep commanding voice. "As well as my own tribe I can now call upon the warriors of the Sacred Moon".

"Can their Tribal Chief be trusted to keep his silence?" came a vexed voice.

"I think so Lieutenant Otto". "He was the fighter lying in the circle".

\#

Ben was still weary and kept sniffing his tunic as the two men rode side by side. "I have found dead squirrels that have smelt better than me" he grumbled softly. "Well, if you returned sooner, you could have had a nice long hot bath".

The guardsman shook his head, staring at the landscape when a thought came to him. "Why am I here,

Sir?, if you do not mind me asking. I would not have been Captain Nicolus first choice on such an adventure".

"True", said the Lieutenant after a short pause. "Alas, if we are successful, we will be tasked to Diore for over a year and all the competent Sergeants are required elsewhere". The young officer smirked as he gazed at his companion. "One of my first duties will be to forge trust and friendships with the Royal family and officers of Diore. You are a good soldier who thinks on his feet and as loyal as a Masters hound. I need someone I can have complete faith in down there".

He stopped to survey the lands around them, pulled a wooden flask from around his neck. Sipping gently, he then reached over to his startled sergeant, who took some sips and handed the flask back with a grateful nod. "We will not laze in their Citadel all the time. Captain Nicolus wants us to explore the Io Desert ourselves, your ways of surviving in unforgiving lands, will be very useful".

"The Io Desert!" blurted Ben nearly falling off Titan."I hear the tribesmen are bloodthirsty beasts that flay strangers alive for merriment"."Which makes me believe they do not care for us very much" he cried in horror.

"Not true, my Captain tells me that when he travelled the Desert long ago, the hospitality of the tribesmen were legendary. They showed him the stars and talked about

17

them in their legends and gave him the best games of chess of any man."

"One moment Sir" spluttered Ben. "The first time I met your Captain Nicolus he saved my neck from that unhinged commander Ursa in Northern Mimas. Said he would send me on patrol through the Io Desert instead of being hanged. I do not think that lunatic would have agreed if he thought I would be playing games and pointing at the stars all night!!".

"Not really how we talk about officers is it Hawks", the Lieutenant replied in a tired manner as he looked around at the fading sky. "We have travelled far, we will camp for the night near to that stream over there. Look after the mounts while I search for some fire wood, tomorrow will be another day".

"Yeah, another day closer to losing my skin!" Ben whispered to himself.

CHAPTER TWO

THE KINGDOM OF DIORE

The guardsman always slept lightly. He silently rose barely before dawn and listened fruitlessly for signs of danger. Kingswood stirred a little later as the small crackling fire woke him from his slumber.

"The rabbits will need a while yet on the fire Sir but you have some fresh water in your flask and some fruit next to your boots". The Lieutenant was wide awake the moment he sat up." I take it the time spent in Callisto honed your already sharp night time skills then?, oh, thank you for the water".

"It is odd how sharp a man can be when the fear of death is hanging over him in perilous lands, Sir".

Eventually the two devoured their breakfast and Kingswood cleared his throat. "You still have the nightmares?" he asked softly starring at the glowing embers of the fire.

"Sorry Sir", answered the guardsman shamefully. "I still see the faces of the dead men from when I patrolled the Swamplands last year".

"No need to be sorry, - how often?".

"Every night I think, I tried drinking ale, made myself sick. Tried practicing so hard I could hardly move to tire myself out but – he shrugged his wide shoulders. "Mostly I see the bandit I mortally wounded with my bow, he always begs me to stop his suffering", his voice was cracking slightly.

Kingswood gave a small sigh as he looked at the forelorn man. "There were other reasons why I wanted to come with me, Ben. I got the glory for helping to stop the Marauders from raiding Almathea. We both know though, your actions that night saved many lives, yes, you have some deadly skills but they are finely balanced by your loyalty and sense of duty. Now enough of these soft words, we have to get to the town of Maxwell in three days. Tell a living soul I gave you real praise and I will flay you alive!" he barked with a grin.

"Sir!, replied Ben with a bigger grin as he sprang to his feet.

The journey was quite relaxing compared to what the two men were usually used to, Ben was now warming to

Kingswood as an officer. He was not arrogant or pompous unlike some officers he had met before. Usually he felt an inclination to run them through with a sword the moment they spoke to him but Lieutenant Kingswood was different. When they were alone he was treated as an equal and the officer even suggested light sword practice when they made camp after resting. Kingswood was indeed an excellent blade, who fought with his sabre as they have been taught in Minmas for centuries, he was very nimble and counter attacked like a lightening bolt. He even insisted that his Sergeant should fight with both his swords all the time. "You cannot pick the rules of a contest in battle!" he chirped constantly.

Three days after they left the border, the men arrived in Maxwell, the guardsman could see most of the town was filled mainly with stables posts and scruffy looking Taverns. Kingswood nodded at a sign hanging from one such Tavern which read" The Drunken Soldier" with a picture of a soldier still holding his musket bending over a wooden barrel being sick.

"They are expecting us here, no need to draw attention to ourselves" he explained as he saw his companion raised eyebrow. "See to the mounts at the stables next door and I will meet you inside. I will take that big parcel your beast of a mount has been carrying for us as well. They are our ceremonial uniforms I had made for us in Almanthea, we have to look well kept if we are invited to any banquets or gatherings."

Ben gave Kingswood a long look. "You know what Lieutenant?, you and Captain Nicolus are very much alike".

"Thank you Sergeant" gushed the officer looking very pleased with himself. "It was not a compliment!!" he muttered under his breath as he led the mounts to the stables.

A short while later they were finishing a heavy tavern supper."I will finish my flagon and go to bed" remarked Kingswood looking tired and worn."I do not mind if you wish to stay down here longer. You probably have not enjoyed yourself for some time!" he added kindly.

He mumbled a befuddled thank you and stood up as the Lieutenant left which drew some glances from around the tables. Ben wondered how he was supposed to have a good time at this place and did not see the generous gesture as it was meant. To him taverns were always dirty, noisy places where the wilds were clean and peaceful. He took a deep gulp of his ale and grimaced". This really tastes like washing water!". He went to check on the mounts and went up to his bed, bored and restless.

#

The next morning Kingswood and Ben woke at dawn, refreshed, they rode away from the Drunken Soldier in good spirits. "I know you were going to give old Tom one of the mounts you won, I thought the code of the Civil Mountain Guard was to keep what you gather?, asked Kingswood with a twinkle in his eye.

"He gave me some useful advice" replied Ben cautiously, he thought best not to talk about the purse of coins right now. The Lieutenant burst out laughing. "I do not mind traditions as long as they are fair and honest".

"You do seem more open minded than most, Sir" said Ben sincerely.

The officer shrugged his shoulders, "like Captain Nicolus, I believe we can all hold onto our customs yet still be unified and strong".

The guardsman was impressed but at the same time very curious where they were heading. "Sir, is it true that Diore has strict laws and has not changed for hundreds of years?".

"They are not as strict as the good folk of Almanthea" grinned Kingswood." The key roles are taken by the aristocracy but they work hard and are greatly loved by their people. It was the Grand prince of Diore; their ruling prince, who made peace with the Io tribesmen many moons ago. Indeed they greatly respected each others culture and beliefs.".

"What are their soldiers like, any good?" the guardsman was always interested in the strengths and weaknesses of armies from other lands.

"They are well trained and well armed, they have sworn to protect the Royal family, their lands and do a pretty good job!. The officers are encouraged to practice hard with the sword and have some excellent instruction".

"Really, this task will seem like heaven for you then Lieutenant!". Ben kept gazing around at the landscape but the only movement came along the old worn road they were travelling on. Merchant caravan after caravan passed them, some brightly painted and rich looking, some so rickety the two were surprised they made it so far. Later in the afternoon, they reached the top of a knoll and Kingswood pointed to some white tall elegant spires in the distance. "The Citadel of Diore" he announced importantly, "the Captain wants us fresh and wide awake when we get there, so we will camp down now and set off early tomorrow".

"I thought poste haste was required for our arrival Lieutenant".

Kingswood gave a knowing smile and a wink, "You will learn one day that a good first meeting of any union always brings it's rewards, Sergeant".

Apart from a lone wolf howling towards the night time sky, the lands were dark and peaceful. Kingswood woke up abruptly as something disturbed the mounts.

"Now be calm and you may live through this, soldier" came a quiet rasping voice in front of the officer. "What do you want?" he commanded, squinting, he looked around for his Sergeant to no avail. "Anything of value you carry, - and your provisions, we do like a good breakfast!" replied the dark figure. He held out a long rusty looking sabre, pointed at the Lieutenant. The dying light of the camp fire danced along the blade.

"There are two saddles with two mounts, so where is your friend?" cried another , much sharper voice. "Behind you!", Ben's dull bladed curved sword was now resting under the robber's throat.

"You careless FOOL!" shouted the first man as he ran at Kingswood, his old sabre held out in front. Still lying on the ground, the officer threw his blanket at his assailants face. Rolling sideways, he rose up swiftly, sword in hand and ran the man through. "I am a Lieutenant now, if you must know" he chirped in an offended tone as the man crumpled to the ground.

"I'LL KILL YOU" screamed the second robber as he span around to face Ben. The guardsman savagely brought his knee up under the man's belt and smashed the hilt of the sword down on the back of his attacker's head as he doubled over.

Without any jubilation, his looked around frantically in the darkness. "There is another one around somewhere Sir, I should have killed this one outright but thought you would want a prisoner!". There was a deathly silence then Kingswood slashed the darkness behind him and as a shrill cry filled the night air, he stepped forward and plunged his sword down, twice, finishing off the stricken figure.

"Your eyes are good to see him" Ben observed in admiration.

"Not really, his breath stank of ale" laughed the officer. "So, - even though I said there was no need to keep watch on Diore's border, you did so anyway?".

"Uh, - yes, Ben answered slowly, Best not take any chances, Lieutenant". Then a thought occurred. "Sir, did you sleep with that sword under your blanket?".

"Best not take any chances Sergeant" echoed Kingswood, his voice full of merriment.

#

The next day, the men set off early as planned, with their prisoner walking briskly ahead of them. His hands bound tightly by rope, the other end was attached to Titan's saddle. Once they left the hills, all they could see were fields of strange vine like plants growing against strips of wood, in the distance there was a large forest barely beyond the Citadel. Ben stared at the trees in peaceful reflection when something caught his eye. "Horsemen, - a patrol, heading towards us, over there" he nodded as he reached for his bow.

"I expected them sooner but they must have most of their soldiers positioned near the Gold River I suppose". The Lieutenant looked down at their bedraggled captive. "Mmmm, that would explain while our friend was free to skulk around. Diore is renowned for it's security and safe passage through it's lands. He finished talking as the patrol rode up to them.

With their bright crimson tunics and black trousers, red feather plumes sprouting from flat black hats and shiny new leather saddles, they made the Almathea City guard look unkept.

"Welcome to Diore" stated the leading soldier, who was short but confident looking, he took off his hat and bowed slightly, showing his shiny shaven head. "May I ask your business here?". The soldiers eyes narrowed on the robber as they spoke.

"We are expected, we are the emissaries from Mimas", Kingswood spoke proudly. I am Lieutenant Kingswood and this is Sergeant Hawks of the Civil Mountain Guard. This man and his friends attacked us last night by our camp fire. The others are next to the road, on the second knoll from here, they will never trouble anyone again".

A big, bushy bearded soldier trotted over and Ben handed the rope to him. The leading man spoke again but gave the robber a withering look as he was dragged past.

"Lewis, Humphries, the second knoll from here, bury them deep!". Two other horsemen exchanged glances at each other but groaned "Yes Sergeant" and galloped away. "My name is Sergeant Usk, I deeply regret you were attacked on Diore soil. We have been expecting you, we are here to escort you to the Citadel".

"We were summoned from other duties, such was the importance" answered Kingswood who saw it as an half-truth at least. "Let us ride and we will be at the Grand Prince's disposal the moment we get there". The patrol wasted little time.

#

The towering bright white Citadel now loomed in front of them as the sergeants chatted away. It was clear Sergeant Usk liked talking and Ben found him to be warm and friendly when he was not scowling at the prisoner running along side them.

"So is it true the Civil Mountain Guard talk to their mounts all the time in the mountains enquired Sergeant Usk", grinning broadly. Ben was about to answer when they passed over a small solid looking stone moat bridge and through the outer wall to the ancient town of Silver.

Ben gazed up at the splendid stone buildings along the main road. Most looked like shops selling their wares but there were also a few taverns.

Unlike the town of Maxwell, these looked grand and well maintained. Even the roads appeared clean and did not smell like a toilet. "Not likely to see The Drunken Soldier around here!" he chuckled.

"A creature of beauty, is she not?" nodded Sergeant Usk up at the Citadel. "The Ruling family did not build it purely as a symbol of wealth, the white limestone is only a shell around thick granite blocks. The many balconies you see all have murder holes and each room next to it has stored inside small cannons with plenty of grape and shot in case of attack. Even our barracks and stables are inside. Great Sergeant Task says a army of a thousand men could not pierce the Citadel and wait until you see the fortifications by the river!. The guardsman felt envy of the pride Usk had for his principality, he never felt respected or felt wanted outside his home town of Jovia.

"Great Sergeant Task" he repeated belatedly, "bet they give him plenty to do" he laughed out loud. Usk suddenly had the fear of the devil in his eyes.

"Would be wise to not to mock his name out loud, Sergeant Hawks, he is the most fearsome adversary a man could meet and is very strict on all matters".

"Great!", cannot wait to meet him", Ben quipped as he rolled his eyes towards the sky.

Two huge high crimson painted doors opened inwards as the patrol trotted on, to be swallowed by the magnificent fortress. As the group came to a second pair of equally imposing doors, Sergeant Usk guided the two guests to the left into a sparely lit corridor.

"We will part company here, Lieutenant Kingswood" he explained politely."We will take your mounts to the stables and look after them well" he smiled and gave a reassuring nod at Ben. "Your prisoner will not be treated so fairly". The big, bearded soldier dragged the robber away and his cries of mercy could still be heard in the distance. The patrol bid farewell and rode off down the vast corridor.

"Lieutenant Kingswood, we have been expecting you, Sir", asked a stocky soldier as he stepped from the shadows. He wore the same crimson tunic and black trousers as the other soldiers but his feather plumed hat seemed to sit awkwardly atop his head. Ben instinctively put himself between this stranger and his officer. "You move well", commended the man, his eyes latched onto the guardsman instantly. Ben stared at this man with unease, although not as tall as the travelling companions, his wide shoulders and broad chest made him look powerful. His light hazel eyes eyes were filled with confidence and his sudden emergence showed he was fleet of foot.

"Great Sergeant Task" reasoned Ben as he stepped to one side so his Lieutenant could see. "It helps, - when I hunt" he added with a wry smile.

"Yess, I see you as a – hunter", Task's eyes fell onto Ben's bow. "I suppose the question is, what do you like to hunt?". He gazed at the guardsman from head to toe. Ben gazed back and opened his mouth to reply when Kingswood gave a slight cough.

"Usually bales of hay to feed that monster of a mount he rides. I do not wish to press you Great Sergeant but if you could show us to our quarters, it would be good to change my uniform before I meet the Citadel Commander".

"Yes, - off course Lieutenant" answered Task slowly still staring at Ben, he then broke his gaze and snapped his heels as he gave a slight bow to the officer. "Your description fits what your Captain Nicolus had written on the parchment, sent in advance. Please follow me". "You are very thorough" observed Kingswood.

"The importance of the Royal family is beyond measure and many ancient secrets are held in the Citadel, Lieutenant, we must be on guard against all threats". He glanced at Ben once more with a vicious smile as a patter of little footsteps came behind them. "I will take you to the officer quarters post haste Lieutenant Kingswood and Marcus here will see to your sergeant.

"The corridors here are like a labyrinth sergeant so this boy will be your shadow at all times". Task's voice now became low and dangerous, "He will be at your call day and night but if you wander around the Citadel without him, I cannot guarantee your well being. Marcus, if you could now take him to the servant quarters".

"The what!! hissed Ben as the Great Sergeant started to climb narrow stone spiral staircase.

"Not now Sergeant" whispered Kingswood as he walked past the guardsman trembling, as he stifled a laugh.

Situated at the base of the Citadel, the corridors leading to the servant quarters were narrow and dark. The lad swiftly led the guardsman to his new quarters and opened the door for him. "You have the room to yourself and a lock was fitted to your door, here is the key". I will bring some food up now but usually the soldiers eat at the canteen. Marcus had been smiling all the time but now looked uneasy. "My room is down the hallway sir, please knock on the door if you require any assistance.

He looked at the boy's face as he asked the question. "I take it Task is serious about you being my shadow?".

Marcus looked up and down the corridor as he spoke softly. "I am afraid he is deadly serious, Sir".

"Yes, thought he was and I am sure he can be very deadly as well. Well, I need to clean my weapons and wait until my - Master summons me!" he chuckled. Do you have a training yard, or room where I can practice with weapons early tomorrow?, no offence but this room looks rather, - compact" he uttered tactfully.

"There is a training hall on this side of the Citadel", his sincere, beaming smile was now fully restored. "I will be here at dawn, goodnight sir".

"Goodnight and please call me Ben".

#

He polished his shiny throwing knives and then started on his swords. When he came to the dull bladed curved sword, he always took his time as he remembered the words of it's former Master, a great warrior. "It does not look much but is one of the best, when needed", Ben thought the remark could have been aimed at him as well, if he kept training hard and not court attention. Although Civil Mountain Guards were hardy souls, they were never known swordsmen. Someone with his swordsmanship and especially his throwing knives would be strung up before you could say murdering assassin!. It was a risk but he liked practicing and liked to think he could make a difference if needed. He polished the wooden handle with a piece of cloth and gripped firmly a grey rounded metal button set in the middle of it. As he twisted it and pulled hard, a small, thin, curved dagger silently slipped out and he carefully cleaned this as well. The previous owner never told of this and when he found out by accident one day, he had the fright of his life!.

Once everything was inspected and cleaned, Ben curled on his straw mattress and tried to find some sleep. He had only one murder hole in his bedroom and he left it un-shuttered. It was draughty but the guardsman felt like the walls were creeping onto him, the soft breeze made him feel at ease.

Eventually he drifted into a slumber but woke up several times, crying out for forgiveness, his body trembling. The second time there was a soft knock at the door and he sprang up gratefully, so not to endure another nightmare.

"Morning, beamed Marcus as he thrust a piece of parchment under Ben's nose.

"Happy little creature aren't you" he exclaimed lightly as he read the note.

It was from Lieutenant Kingswood and it was clear the officer was in a jovial mood the night before. "One of the officers here has offered to show me around the Citadel and town defences. As I will not require my servant! in the morning, you can spend the time as you wish. I will meet you in the Grey Falcon Tavern at midday. DO NOT TALK TO ANY OFFICERS AND KEEP AWAY FROM GREAT SERGEANT TASK!!."

"Very jovial, you upper class choir boy "then he realised he still had company. "Could you take me to training hall now Marcus?, I need to work some aggression off". Slipping on a white worn looking tunic, he swiftly put his boots on and grabbed both swords. The Citadel was vast and the passages did indeed seem like a labyrinth. Marcus bounded up some stone steps like a playful puppy but Ben could not help wondering if the boy was lost, as they kept heading upwards, further from the ground.

After a while they reached a big heavy iron door. Ben wrenched it open to see some battlements with heavy black cannons pointing over them. Jaw open, he looked around to see a wide flagstone area away from the edge with an array of weapons hanging from the main outer wall. There was only a tired looking man on duty sitting on the battlements, he eyed the guardsman uniform with casual interest but gave a polite nod and resumed his vigil.

Marcus smiled happily and trotted over to join the sentry as Ben began to loosen off his taut muscles, still gazing at the wall of weapons. The normal guardsman in Eastern Mimas did not receive much sword training. This guardsman however, while on patrol in the borderlands had stumbled across some men who had. This changed his approach to combat and practice forever.

With his dull curved sword in one hand and his straight plain looking sword in the other, he slowly and deliberately honed his skills. Each precise move in his mind was to block an attackers blade or to strike an opponent down. He was working up quite a sweat when he realised more eyes were now watching him.

He looked up to see two bare chest men in black trousers staring at him. "This must be one of our distinguished guests from Mimas, David" grunted the taller man.

"I did not think they needed to practice Ron" replied the slightly shorter man mischievously, his hairy belly hanging over his trousers.

"My name is Sergeant Ben Hawks from the civil Mountain Guard" he explained panting heavily, standing at ease.

"Civil Mountain Guard?, then you do need the practice" sniggered Ron as he glanced at his friend and made a mock neighing impression of a horse. Ben was proud but knew Kingswood would not want any trouble.

"Oh, somehow I manage. You look ready to train so I will leave you to it" he said politely as he stepped towards the Iron door.

"At least he does not look like a dandy, like his officer we saw last night" sneered David. "I think the wenches at the Taverns could best him". "For that matter, I think he could be a wench from the Taverns!" both men laughed deeply. Ben froze and took a long deep breath.

"I would say let us not say something that we may regret later but alas, - that barge has now sailed" he smiled but his voice was cold and unwavering.

"Perhaps you think we may need to be taught some manners, horse talker" snarled Ron as walked briskly to the weapons wall and grabbed two thick wooden quarter staves."Here, he barked as he threw one at the guardsmans head. Instantly dropping his swords, Ben right hand plucked the flying staff from the air and walked away from his weapons to a clear space.

"One at a time or both together?" he enquired in a testing voice. He had wanted to do the proper thing and leave but now desired strongly to treat these disrespectful halfwits a lesson.

"Me first!" spat David, Ron handed him the other staff and gave him a knowing nod then the soldier walked over and faced Ben, his fat fingers gripping the wooden pole tightly.

"Any rules?" asked Ben as he took a stance and examined this unfamiliar weapon. "Do not get struck" grunted David and he lunged forward with a cry. Ben was still judging the weight and balance as the end of a quarterstaff jabbed into his midriff. Grimacing in pain he back away instinctively and raised his arms straight, blocking a hard downward strike to his head. He was now alert and vengeful, when his opponents knee came up viciously. Ben stepped back once more and brought his staff down hard on it with a crunch and flicked the end of his weapon across the man's jaw. The heavy man fell to the floor screaming in pain as his Ron looked on dumbfounded, snatched up the staff and grinned evilly.

"MY TURN" roared Ron as he leapt over his stricken friend and struck blow after blow at his opponent's body. This man was much stronger and the well aimed blows nearly knocked the staff from Ben's hands. Teeth clenched, he raised the pole above his head and angled it as the next strike was deflected wide. Sliding forward on the smooth stone flagstones, he thrust the end of the quarterstaff into Ron's belly and then swung the pole low, catching his leading leg. With a yelp of pain the soldier crumpled down next to his friend in a heap.

"I was right, you do move well", came a hard voice behind the guardsman.

"I can move when someone is trying to bash my head in!" croaked Ben, getting his breath back. He turned around to Great Sergeant Task staring at him coldly.

Wearing only his black trousers and boots, his torso was a block of muscle and looked like it had been chiselled from stone.

"I sent David and Ron up here for extra practice, they are very loyal but getting soft." The Great Sergeant rubbed his chin with great thought as he spoke. "The stories I hear of the Civil Mountain Guard do you no justice, Sergeant Hawks". He bounded over to the fallen quarterstaff, without thinking he put his foot on it, rolled backwards and flicked it up into his hands with ease. "It would be a privilege if we could practice together, perhaps I may learn something" he chuckled with a devilish glint in his eyes. He snapped his fingers hard but kept his gaze on Ben. "David, Ron, to the side, NOW!". The two red faced soldiers limped towards the wall but David shot an evil smile at the guardsman as he did so.

"This may be unwise Great sergeant, we are allies, I do not want to cause any ill feeling".

"Please, indulge me" Task said firmly, "I want allies I can trust in the cauldron of battle". With that the Great Sergeant gave a low bow, his eyes firmly on the guardsman. Ben did the same and both men stepped back in a fighting stance, front leg nearly straight, back leg bent, quarterstaffs at the ready. The guardsman once more slid along the stone flagstones, jabbing the end of his staff at Tasks face. Smiling, the Great Sergeant slid backwards, his head bobbing from side to side. With one deft move he flicked his attackers staff to the side and struck him hard in the belly. As he groaned in pain, Task brought the end of his staff up onto the guardsman's chin. Dazed and unbalanced he fell onto the hard floor but kept his body moving as he rolled backwards and swiftly stood to his feet. A knowing look spread across Task's face as he smiled broadly."Do that a lot when you hunt deer?". Ben said nothing as he sprang at his adversary with a snarl of defiance, he held the end of his staff as he swung it around his head, then crouched low as he brought it down hard on Task's foot.Cursing loudly with pain and surprise, Task half-limped, half-charged at his opponent with a look of thunder. Blow after blow smashed into Ben's staff, as he felt the sheer power shudder through his whole body. Then a loud "CRAA-CK" echoed around the practice floor as he found himself holding a piece of the quarterstaff in either hand. Another blow struck his chest with such force that he slid backwards onto his knees. A animal rage flooded his body as without thinking both sharp pieces of timber were now aimed at the Great Sergeant's wide chest. With a huge battle cry he leapt forward as a familiar voice rang out.

"That is enough practice for today, Hawks!" ordered lieutenant kingswood in a loud stern voice.

"At ease Great Sergeant" ordered a shrill voice. Both men stood to attention bolt upright. Ben then realised he still had the pieces of quarterstaff in his hands. He quickly threw them behind him as if nobody had seen them.

"With men at arms like this standing shoulder to shoulder, how can we fail!" exclaimed the shrill voice again. Ben could see a tall, lean, young faced officer standing next to the red faced Kingswood.

"Quite, Lieutenant Pindar" his officer replied, shaking his head slowly to his sergeant. "I want you cleaned up when I see you in the town later, Hawks. I trust you will be still be able to walk there" he added reproachfully. Painfully he followed Marcus to the barrack washrooms, the young lad still bounced around and he nearly lost him three times on the way there. After a relaxing soak in the warm baths, Ben felt much better. His chin had stopped bleeding and his whole jaw felt sore and tender. His chest and belly had felt as if Titan had trampled underfoot. He felt dejected as Marcus had appeared once more with a thick brown towel.

"May I say you were very brave, Sir, back there. Most folk refuse to practice with Great sergeant Task and those who do, go down a lot more swiftly than you did today!."

"I told you, you can call me Ben" he said, holding his chest in discomfort, "but thank you".

"Beg your pardon, Sir, you are very kind but there are rules we must follow in the Citadel". He gazed at the fair haired boy with blue eyes twinkling with innocence, who now looked so serious. "I understand, the last thing I would want is to get you in trouble.

You do the Citadel a service, your father must be very proud".

"Never knew my father, Sir, he was killed by smugglers when I was small, he was a soldier like you".

The guardsman cursed to himself, "I am sure he was a better soldier than me" he smiled weakly. "Here, may I have that towel now please, I best get dressed and have some breakfast, could show me to the canteen in a while?",

Marcus now seemed happy once more, "If I may be bold sir, it would be as well to escort you back to your room. I shall bring some food up, it is quiet but it would not look good for the other soldiers to see you like this".

Ben smiled broadly, "You have a wise head on those shoulders, I will submit to your wisdom".

After the best breakfast he had ever had by quality and the huge portion that covered the plate, Marcus led Ben to the barracks stable. "Are all the mounts from Mimas as big as Titan?, he enquired in awe, as he fetched a stool so he could stand on tiptoe and pat the beast on the neck.

"Not really, he does devour a lot of hay and has a fondness of cabbages and carrots. Ben could see the sparkle in the boys eyes and Titan seemed to love the extra attention as well. "Here", the guardsman said as he rummaged in his chest pocket for his purse. "If you do have time, would you get some and treat him from time to time. Anything left, keep for yourself, you are doing me a favour, he means the world to me", he said honestly giving the lad some coins.

"You mean that?, off course sergeant Hawks" he gushed brightly. Shortly afterwards, Marcus gave the guardsman a short tour of the town. The boy was an excellent guide and explained in great detail how the town prospered for over five hundred years. "Folk feel safe here when they come to trade or rest on the way to Almanthea, here, I will show why". Forever smiling, Marcus trotted down to the southern town wall and again bounced up the chiselled stone steps towards the top of the wall. Ben was astounded to see the great Gold river with vast grassy plains and a few knolls beyond it. The wide slow flowing stretch of water did indeed sparkle like grains of gold under the bright sun and the guardsman struggled not to become entranced by the beauty. "Here is the reason everyone used to feel safe here – but Great Sergeant Task says it is the peace treaty that protects the region", the boy pointed in front of the river. "Thought he would be the last person to want peace!", Ben muttered under his breath with a twinkle in his eyes.

Ben looked down on a mass of thick walls tipped by wide battlements with three rows of cannon. The last row only contained four cannon but they were spread far apart and each were longer than three carts tied together and the barrels were large enough for the guardsman to lie in. He gave a sharp blow of breadth through his teeth. "I think those monsters could blow a barge to pieces on the far side of the river" he gasped. He then turned and held out his hand. "Thank you Marcus, you have been very helpful".

"Just doing my job, I will now take you to the Lieutenant" blurted out the boy. His cheeks turned a deep red colour as he grasped the sergeants hand tightly. He did not often receive praise from the soldiers.

CHAPTER THREE

THE MISTS OF DIPLOMACY

He sat at a table in the Grey Falcon Inn, and held a hanker chief to his chin to stem the bleeding. "With men of arms like this, standing to shoulder, how can we fail?" murmured Kingswood with an irritable tone. "How can you still be bleeding??, he hit you with a quarterstaff not a axe!.".

"I must have rubbed it somehow and it started again" Ben answered with a sheepish look. "I do not think he trusts me".

"Really" replied the Lieutenant in a mocking voice. "You prance around their training floor with two swords, beat up two of their soldiers then manage to hold off one of their finest in practice!". "In Eastern Mimas, the Civil Mountain Guard are hardly known for their fondness of hard training with the sword. What are you going to tell him, you were taught unique fighting skills by mysterious slavers in the swamps of Callisto?".

"He is one of their finest?" echoed the guardsman with a pleased look.

"Yeah, well, they say he is far better with a sword so try not to get any delusions of grandeur. Are you going to drink that ale or merely bleed in it all afternoon?". "To be honest Sir I am still a little taken a back. No officer has ever bought me a drink before, are you certain we are not breaking a law or something?". Kingswood tried to keep a stern look on his face but gave a half smile at this remark, then became serious again.

"When I jested to Lieutenant Pindar that you would be more likely practicing instead of enjoying Diore's hospitality, he suggested we go to the training floor at once. The folk here think, with good reason that we have abandoned them, not everybody will be happy to see us here". Kingswood face now looked less serious and he looked around the Tavern as he spoke softly."I heard from a little bird that you were baited to fight, the soldiers said some - harsh words?."

"I tried to walk away sir but they said-", he calmed himself, "as you say sir, some folk are not happy to see us".

The lieutenant looked at his sergeant kindly,"some good did come out of your display this morning. The people of Diore were expecting a couple of pompus old fools as their emissaries. To have a so called hero of Almanthea and a virile sergeant like you at his side shows that Mimas holds great importance in this alliance. His voice dropped to a whisper. "To have someone like you to watch my back will be a comfort over the next few days" he smiled, "We have an early start tomorrow, I cannot say much but be prepared for anything!.

The two soldiers talked jovially about their impressive surroundings at the citadel and what they have seen so far of the town and the surrounding landscape.

"I must be off now, I have been invited to dine with the royal household tonight" the Lieutenant remarked as he stood up and puffed out his chest with a mock gesture of importance. "See what you can find out from the locals about the tribesman and the lands around here, to be forewarned is to be forearmed as I keep telling you!". He put some coins down next to Ben's pitcher, mouthed" the next one is on me" and glided through the crowd into the street.

Ben could not believe how he had fallen on his feet to get such an officer as Kingswood as he casually looked around the tavern to see someone he could strike up a conversation with.

#

He was up and dressed in his black guard uniform when Marcus knocked to show him where the dining hall was for breakfast. The boy was his same friendly, bouncy self and Ben wondered if he could bottle his secret and become rich on it.

The hall was massive and row after row of long polished tables covered the floor, great shafts of light flooded in from three huge stain glass windows and the vaulted ceiling loomed high above him.

A small cough told him where to find Lieutenant Kingswood. Ben sat down next to him and could see the officer had a good time last night. "Good morning Lieutenant, I presume the ale which was served at the supper had a pleasing taste?" he enquired quietly as he glanced around the table.

"Being a officer I do what I must" he smiled gleefully, "it also helped me through the night, if I had a coin every time someone told me that Minmas should do more to keep the peace...".

He looked vexed as he whispered, their table was empty bar the two of them but he was still very careful. "We leave for the desert this morning, a twenty strong party including the two of us, led by Princess Marie herself". Ben exaled sharply in surprise. "It will be a peace mission" continued Kingswood, "we are to meet one of their leaders on top of his knoll camp near to the river".

"Well, it will be a massacre if they have misjudged it!" warned the guardsman gravely.

"We are guests here, we follow their orders". Ben leaned back in his chair with a big shrug of his wide shoulders and a weak smile.

"And I, follow yours Sir".

Later that morning, the column had already disembarked from a large sailing barge. The soldiers were greeted by an advanced group of their own and everyone were looking over their muskets as Ben saw the Princess for the first time. Tall, angelic with yellow hair cut short over her shoulders, she was pale skinned but her cheeks were red and even the dour brown dress she wore could not mask her beauty.

"That is Princess Marie?, I gather you spent plenty of time talking to her at the supper.

"Watch your words" whispered Kingswood as he glanced to see if anyone had heard. "She is loved by the whole of Diore".

"I can see why, OW!".

"If you must know, snarled the officer as he lifted his foot of his sergeant's, "we discussed the council of Almanthea and the growth of our armies".

"Really, nothing else?" Ben said with a cheeky grin. He could see that Kingswood now had red cheeks and was determined to enjoy this.

"Remember your place, Hawks and what do you know of women?, Hell!, Task is coming over here now".

"I think he wants to ask me where he can buy a bow like mine, he has been staring at it all morning".

"Everything well Lieutenant?" asked the great sergeant, his unwavering gaze fixed firmly on the guardsman.

"OH yes, great sergeant, thank you, we were sharing our knowledge on the tribesmen", Kingswood replied.

"They are a tough race in a tough land" exclaimed Task, flexing his powerful shoulders. "Their warriors fight with honour and are strong and skilful with the blade, it takes two normal soldiers to match one warrior in battle. Attacking a caravan and setting fire to a barge, makes no sense, they desire only to be left alone as masters of their own lands. Sergeant Hawks, -may I ask you if you are on the right side?. With your curved sword and tribesmen bow, you do resemble one of them".

"Well at least when the fighting does begin, I will be able to bring some of them down with me" he smiled through his gritted teeth as he spoke.

"You must excuse Hawks, great sergeant, he is a brave guardsman and resourceful in battle, alas talking to folk was not a skill he could practice while patrolling the mountains on his own." The officer's eyes widened and shook his head slightly as he too now fixed a gaze on his sergeant.

"It matters little, as you say, there are not many folk in the mountains". He looked towards the Princess and it suddenly dawned on Ben that perhaps he was not the only soldier who was given advice about how to speak to allies this morning. The stonic great sergeant took a step closer and lowered his voice as he spoke. "Prince Friedrich was the royal who made peace with the tribesmen long ago. He cannot travel now with his ill health but the Princess wants to keep that peace at all cost!!"

Task then gave a sly grin which looked almost demonic on his face. "I am no fool Gentlemen, our sailing barge has the biggest cannons it can carry hidden from view under drapes. The slightest smell of trouble and they have orders to open fire".

"I like your thinking, great sergeant" remarked Ben honestly, "what is their range though?".

"Not your concern" snapped Task, he clenched his right hand and made a strange noise has he remembered the speech about diplomacy from his Prince". He nodded over his shoulder, "they have offered one of their warriors as a guide so best not give away our advantage" he whispered as he strolled away to bellow his frustrations at some of his men.

"He does look tough" agreed Kingswood. The man was walking towards the column, leading his mount behind him. Covered in white robes, his muscles bulged through them and a small narrow black beard hung from his wide square jaw.

"He has got good taste" observed Ben as he saw the mans bow hanging from his saddle.

Eventually the column was ready and set off slowly from the river bank. The soldiers rode in pairs as Ben gazed at the view. "Flat grassy plain with a few knolls before that ridge, hardly a barren desert!". The disappointment was clear on the guardsman's face.

"Merchants always tell tales of the harsh lands they travelled through so they can barter a higher price for their wares", explained Kingswood.

"We seem to be heading for that last knoll by the ridge" said Ben with a vexed look, that will take us beyond the range of any cannon".

"What did you find out about the tribesmen at the Grey Falcon" enquired Kingswood, who was now looking quite vexed himself.

"Most of the warriors are giants, if killed under a full moon they come back to life, oh, they can put an arrow in the eye of a wolf at a hundred paces.

What?, I do not deserve a look like that Lieutenant, the place was full of drunk locals, one even tried to kiss me!". "They must have been drunk, I hear even Titan refuses your advances!" laughed the lieutenant, then cleared his throat. "I heard that they travel around these lands in their tents because they choose to, their scholars are wiser than ours, their medicine really does heal and in a battle, you want them on your side". The officer now looked at his pale companion. "It will be fine Ben, but I am glad the soldiers carry only the best muskets".

"I am glad we have Task" said the guardsman under his breath.

The sun seemed to get hotter among the huge deep blue skies as they neared the knoll. You see anything". "No, wait – some tribesmen are coming around the foot of the knoll from the right. Now there are some from the left!"."Perhaps a guard to welcome the Princess?, ventured Kingswood trying to reassure himself.

"Perhaps" said Ben as he reached for his bow.

"At ease, we do not want to worry anyone".

"Too late for that" grinned Ben nervously as his hand drew away from his weapon. Standing on his stirrups Kingswood could see the "Guard" had now formed a straight line in front of them.

"Twenty of them, same number as our column, all their faces are covered up, no banners or emblems to announce their tribe" reported Ben on his superior perch, his eyes searching for the smallest detail. A rasping, booming voice rang out across the plain.

"SOLDIERS OF DIORE, THERE IS NO NEED FOR BLOOD TO BE SPILT. WE BELONG TO

NO TRIBE. WE ARE ONLY MEN WHO WISH THE IO LANDS TO BE GREAT ONCE MORE. LAY DOWN YOUR ARMS AND SURRENDER, NO HARM WILL COME TO YOU OR YOUR PRINCESS.

"Does not want much does he?".

"Quiet Sergeant, oh, - and sergeant, you can grab your bow now".

Suddenly, everything happened at once. Lieutenant Pindar gave a shrill command to Task who roared out orders to the men. "SHIELD PLAN NOW!!", the column instantly peeled away in two halves, spreading out to form their own straight line separating the tribesmen from Task, Pindar, kingswood, Hawks and the Princess. As the soldiers halted in position, they swiftly got to the ground and readied their muskets behind their mounts. Lieutenant Pindar took his position behind his men when Ben heard a noise he recognised.

"GET YOUR HEADS DOWN!" he screamed, MOVE!!". Cries of death hung in the air as a cloud of black shafted arrows fell among the soldiers. Kingswood yelped in pain as an arrow plunged into his thigh and two more struck Titans huge saddle. "Lets get you to that hollow over there sir!" yelled Ben as he grabbed the reins of Kingswood mount.

They had barely moved when Tasks voice screamed a warning. "WARRIORS ON HORSEBACK BREAKING THE LINE, PROTECT THE PRINCESS!!"

Without hesitation, Kingswood slapped Ben's hand from his reins and galloped towards the fray. Cursing wildly, the guardsman chased after his lieutenant.

The sound of musket fire still filled the air as the fighting became desperate. The mount of the Princess had been felled by arrows. Task had jumped from his mount and took on two warriors still on horseback, as she slowly got to her feet. Ben looked around to see the remaining soldiers were locked in a grim battle. The men were well drilled and gallant but the tribal warriors gleefully engaged them in personnel combat. Task impaled one attacker and heard the Princess issued a warning and fired at the second with a small silver handled pistol. At such a close distance, the shot hit the man in the belly and he stumbled to the ground.

"Keep them at bay as long as you can!" ordered Kingswood as he rode over to the Princess and pulled her up onto his mount behind him.

"They will be alright, who will look after us?" jested the guardsman darkly as he nocked his bow.

He slowed his breathing and his eyes narrowed on eight warriors now riding hard towards them. His first arrow struck the leading man square in the chest and as he fell, He plucked another arrow from his quiver. It plunged into the shoulder of another warrior who kept charging on as Titan reared up without warning then crashed to the ground. Thrown from the saddle, he rose unsteadily to his feet, his bow and a third arrow which he barely managed to snatch, were still in his grasp. With a swift glance he could see a black shaft sticking from Titans shoulder. His face a mask of rage, he looked on as a warrior leapt from his mount, sword in hand. As the remaining five horsemen charged past, he roared a curse, turned and released his arrow straight into the back of one of them. Feeling sick and groggy, he glanced for his quiver, only to see half of it was crushed under his stricken mount. The warrior now ran forward, his dark eyes filled with excitement for the forthcoming fight. The bloody curved sword sliced the air towards Bens throat as swift with fear, the guardsman rolled to the ground and rose, both swords drawn. This man, as tall as Ben, was much broader and his second blow came down sharply at his opponents head. Crossing his blades high to block this powerful strike, he was rewarded by a kick to the belly. Gasping for air, he rolled around the earth, dodging his assailants murderous blows, only to hear more mounts approaching.

With two on his mount, Kingswood knew they were not going to be swift enough. She held her arms tightly around his waist but he was taken back how calm the Princess was.

"We must do this again sometime" she jested in his ear. Glancing around Kingswood could see the chasing horsemen were spread out so there was no use in Task fighting a rearguard, the other warriors would simply fly past him to claim their prize. The sound of charging hooves filled his ears as thoughts and ideas clouded his mind. He could feel his own mount tiring and wondered how long they would last if they made a stand. He was wounded but it was clear they wanted Princess Marie alive so they may have an advantage there. His pistol was loaded and they had Task who by what he had heard was worth three soldiers. He shook his head, cursing, he had never encountered men in battle like this before - , then something stole his attention in the distance, there was a crack of thunder and he could see three dirty puffs of smoke appear from the river. Three cannon balls flew over their heads and landed a few paces behind the chasing pack in a deafening explosion of black cloud, followed by cries of agony

Kingswood turned to see the horsemen were now covered in a thick, black, choking mist, only two mounts emerged, one mount was by itself without a rider and the other carried a tall bloodied man. Task was struggling in vain to control his panic stricken mount as the warrior tore past him, waving his red bladed sword.

"Stop" ordered Princess Marie in Kingswood's ear.

"Your Highness, it is not safe yet", "I commanded you to stop" she repeated, still calmly but with some added steel to her tone. With a grunt of displeasure, he slowed his mount, turned around to face their pursuer and stopped. Reaching for his pistol, his head was pushed to one side as a musket ball struck the warrior in his throat. The mans eyes flickered in rage at his own carelessness, then rolled up towards the heavens as he slid heavily from his saddle, dead. Kingswood could hardly hear in his right ear as he looked at the Princess. This time she held a much bigger pistol with dull grey metal barrel and tarnished looking brown handle, her arm was still outstretched and shaking but Kingswood thought this was with anger rather than fear.

"Yes, we wanted a prisoner but my mind is not clear, we will get back to the barge now gentlemen".

Both men exchanged looks and glanced back at the now crimson faced Princess whose eyes still glowered at the tall grassy knoll in the distance. They rode hard towards the barge, both were confident that this was not the time to disagree with the lady.

#

Back on the barge, Kingswood was having his wound seen to in the Captains private quarters as Princess Marie strode up and down, her face still red, staring hard at the floor to find answers. Task was in the corner of the cabin, leaning against the wall, arms folded and in deep thought.

"I led us into a trap??, they are the – most graceful of hosts, their honour means the life to them, the leader of the Sacred moon and his father before him, always understood the peace and respected our family who tried to maintain it", she exclaimed in a high voice, shaking her head as she fought back from crying.

"Why cover their faces?, why did they not display any banners or emblems?, they are proud, men, - " Task muttered and looked up. "They do not want us to know which tribe they belong to but why?, they must know this will be seen as an act of war by everyone in the desert lands".

"Someone looking to gain power but not ready to show his cards yet?, said Kingswood slowly. Aahh!, that needle nearly went through me" he complained lightly to the old man sewing up his wound. "Sorry, I am a little vexed myself" he added with a half grimace, half smile to the physician.

"I will come back to bandage the wound and you must rest". You will have a nice scar there once it heals", the man smiled and nodded the Princess.

"I will be covered in them like my bloody sergeant soon" Kingswood grumbled, inspecting the arrowhead that impaled his thigh.

"So an arrow in your thigh does not stop you but a needle makes you yelp in pain?"smiled the Princess, welcoming the distraction. The young lieutenant tried to laugh but cried out in pain once more. "You were very brave, lieutenant, you helped save my life, that is a debt that will never be forgotten". I regret your sergeant fell in battle".

"That is our duty your Highness",

Kingswood painfully sat upright on the bed and gave a deep nod of thanks to the physcian as he left the cabin.

"Great sergeant Task, any chance that sergeant Hawks is still alive?".

Task cleared his throat and raised an eyebrow to the Princess. "Sometimes the warriors do not kill the men they best", he started slowly, "These are men they deem to be unworthy opponents, they get them to wash their garments, feed the animals and so forth. Sergeant Hawks,- despite my misgivings of the man, would never be counted as such. The tribal warriors would see being slain in battle as a grand honour for bravery".

Kingswood's head rolled back as he stared up at the ceiling. "Then he is dead!, he knew I was wounded, he put an arrow in the back of one of the warriors to give our escape a fighting chance".

"I said to Ben it was a comfort to have someone like him watching my back – and he did! ". He gave a snarl and hurled the arrowhead hard against the cabin wall.

CHAPTER FOUR

WHO KNOWS WHO THE GHASTLY HAND OF DEATH TOUCHES NEXT

Muqrins huge bare back, distorted and flexed as he lifted the heavy bladed axe above his head and swung it hard into the thick tree trunk, fixed firmly in the hard, stony ground. Again and again with an animal like roar, he smashed into his favourite target, spraying big splinters of wood in all directions.

A tall gangly looking man approached his master and bowed low to the ground. His white robes flowed loosely around him as he stood up straight. His thin, worn face, kept staring at the ground. "My Master, I do not mean to interrupt your practice but Darius is here as you wished".

"Thank you Farouk, could you leave us please", the big man was now breathing heavily as he carried on slicing chunks off the trunk, "Murqrin the Overpowerer!, my friend, good to see you still have the strength of two oxen!", the newcomer croaked. Standing to Murqrin's shoulder, it was clear Darius had not fought himself for a very long time. His bulging, bloodshot eyes looked similar to that of a toads. His long brown beard flowed down to his belly that his brown robes clung around. A tall pale faced confident looking man stood next to him, he sneered at the back of Farouk, then casually turned to his front, his black robes did not match his short golden hair and it was clear he felt uncomfortable in them.

"Darius, thank you for coming so swiftly, how is the White Princess?, well cared for?, after all, she is our guest". Murqrin kept attacking his target as if his life depended on it, he stopped briefly to wipe his forehead with the back of his giant paw like hand.

Darius himself was now also sweating profusely and coughed nervously as he spoke. "The- the ambush did not go as expected" he blurted. "The soldiers of Diore were very resourceful, they did not head for the hollow to regroup as we expected, they - they even had a barge full of cannons waiting, we suffered losses-". "AARRRHH!!, CRA-AACK, Murgrin gave a bellowing roar and shattered the trunk with an almighty downward blow.

He turned to face the trembling Darius. He spoke softly yet trembled with rage. "You had -surprise, you picked- your own men, your little creature next to you chose the tactics – and still they slipped through your fingers??" he growled menacing.

Darius cowered as he stammered. "It was still a good victory, an army column from Diore destroyed in the Io desert!, we will be respected in Charon and feared in Diore and the lands of Mimas.

"I should still have you staked out for the scavangers!!, there is much more to lose here than your precious stones and shiny garments.. I cannot appear weak to our – –friends. You", Murqrin pointed his axe at the black clad man. "Look in my direction once more and I will split you down the middle, go for a walk!, I wish to speak to your master alone!". Darius nodded sharply and the man gave a short bow and turned and walked away, without saying a word.

"A ruler to be, should show compassion" conceded Murqrin slowly, his eyes glancing at the knolls in the far distance. "You have prisoners?".

"Yes gulped Darius, glad he was still standing, "they will not last the week and I promise they will not speak to anyone".

"I expect not, where you will send them", the big man now allowed himself a thin smile. "Is he – still there?, still alive?" he lowered his voice and looked around the camp as he spoke.

"Yes but not for long, as I have predicted, he is suffering in mind and body, he will perish soon enough with the soldiers".

"You should never have taken him there". "Make it happen, spare no effort, send your little creature in there as well, he likes to wash his hands in the blood of others, unleash whatever beasts you must but they will be all dead by the end of the week". "You helped me a long time ago Darius and I am thankful for that, yet fail me once more old friend and I will personally send you to the real Underworld". "Now leave me, I need to practice, Farouk!, my sword!.

#

Ben groaned loudly as he woke to be blinded by the late afternoon sun. His head throbbed madly, as he struggled to sit up, only to face thick rounded wooden bars. "Ah sergeant, you had us all worried for a moment, thought you would not wake up". Lieutenant Pindar spoke brightly but the guardsman could see the officer had bloodied his uniform and there was no air of swagger around the officer.

"Sir" he muttered as he tried to stand up but instead fell back heavily on his backside.

"Here, have some water and I will see to you wounds" said sergeant Usk in his usual gleeful voice. Ben painfully cranked his neck around to see his fellow sergeant with a battered face, kneeling next to him with a leather flask of water in one hand and clean bandages in the other.

"You look even more handsome Usk, thought I was dead, how many more made it?".

"Only the four of us" he said gravely and leaned sideways so the big bearded soldier could be seen. "That is Karl, the remnants of the column got surrounded, at least the Princess escaped" he added.

"Yet they seemed quite keen to capture us once we were bested" exclaimed the lieutenant looking befuddled. While you were sleeping, the guards supplied us with fresh water, bandages and as you can see, they have even put veils over the top of this cage to give us some shade".

"That is good of them, perhaps they want to sell us?" Ben asked, darkly. As he spoke he glanced around. They were in a big wooden cage on a cart, he could see there were more carts in front and behind them, filled with men.

"Perhaps they want to give us back to Diore as an act of goodwill" , offered Karl who now felt as he should be saying something.

"After they have ambushed a peaceful mission?, which they clearly want to remain a mystery?" said the officer in an exasperated high pitched tone. Karl went back to pretending to inspect the cage bars. Lieutenant Pindar was scowling and looked at the veil, then the guards on horseback as they escorted the huge cart.

#

As the afternoon grew on, the soldiers could see the landscape had now become barren and rocky. When dusk came and brought a cool breeze with it, Ben could see they were heading for a mountain not far away. It was not as tall as the ones he was used to seeing in Eastern Mimas but this one looked dark and quite wide and stuck out from the surrounding land like a bad scar. Eventually when they reached it, the tribesmen followed a wide trail downwards. The soldiers stared in disbelief as they carried on through the mouth of an enormous cavern. Flaming torches hung from the walls and brightly burning iron baskets lined their path onwards. The carts holding the prisoners lurched to a sudden stop as the tribesmen came to a halt.

"Out" snapped one of the hard faced warriors as he released the chains holding the cage door. Stiff, sore and befuddled, the men jumped down onto the hard, rock floor. Encircled by warriors, pushed and threatened in a tongue they did not understand, they were led down a wide rough looking wooden ladder. Glancing around Ben could see they were standing in a huge circular shape hole. Hundred paces long with a flat but uneven rocky surface and steep jagged walls.

"There is dried blood all over the floor and look,-scorched marks on the rocks around the edge" exclaimed Lieutenant Pindar, his keen eyes straining through the dim light.

"This place reeks of death" observed the guardsman in a vexed voice as he gazed at a plump bearded man standing at the top of the ladder, flanked by two very dangerous looking warriors.

"My name is Darius" the man declared gleefully in a clear echoing tone, he wore a large rich green waist coat that still clung around his midriff.. "The ancients believed the Underworld was where arcane beasts roomed, lorded over by demonic souls. It was the gateway to hell and is still the same today!. "Who knows who the ghastly hand of death will touch next".

"You really do love your own voice" Ben muttered as a warrior swiftly shoved him in the back.

Darius carried on, "This is an arena where the most infamous and feared warriors fight. If you win ten contests, - you walk free with a bag of gold in one hand and the sword of champions in the other. If you lose, he paused with a big heartless smile cutting across his wide flabby face, "your life will be no more and your soul lost in hell forever".

"Well, that is good to know!" spat Ben who could not care when he died at this moment.

The same warrior raised his sword only for Darius to sharply raise his hand and the warrior stopped abruptly. "You, what is your name?, " he enquired curiously.

"I am Sergeant Hawks of the Civil Mountain Guard" came the answer loudly, trying to appear braver than he now felt.

"Well, the festivities will commence tonight, watched by a crowd paying for the pleasure". The voice of Darius was now edged and there was evil in his eyes. "- And you will be the first to fight, my careless, talking friend!".

"Outstanding sergeant" whispered Lieutenant Pindar in Ben's ear, "really outstanding".

The prisoners were pushed roughly towards a dark part of the arena. Two of the warriors lit several iron fire baskets to unveil two large wooden doors with black iron spikes protruding from it. One of them slowly slid a heavy wooden bolt to one side as the other pulled a massive iron ring, opening the thick doors. All wearing vexed faces the men were ushered inside and as the last one entered, the doors slammed behind him and the heavy wooden bolt once more scraped back into place.

#

Hearing a knock on the door of his chamber, Kingswood called for the person to come in. Lying on his back, doing nothing was torturing the Lieutenant. He knew though that when events started to move, they would move swiftly and he needed to rest and heal as swiftly. Wearily raising his head up expecting to see a servant he was shocked to see Princess Marie glide into the chamber in an ordinary looking light white dress barely covering her ankles.

"Your -your- Highness" he stammered, he grunted in pain as he tried to sit up. "I was not expecting you".

"Please do not excite yourself Lieutenant, you are wounded ", she offered kindly. Her palm of her hand gestured at him to stay how he was, her soft gaze was disarming until he released he was not wearing his tunic and he frantically tried to pull his bed sheet to his shoulders. "There is no need to cover for me, it is not the first time I have seen the chest of a man" she stopped, clenched her fists and her cheeks went a darker red, then she smiled and gave a little laugh.

"The shadow of war hangs over this land and I am vexed that my words do not come out properly".

Now Kingswood gave a little laugh and felt at ease but then asked an important question that he knew would end the jovial mood. "What did Prince Friedrich make of the ambush, your Highness?".

"As one would expect he did not believe it at first, if I was not there, I would not have believe it" she added faintly, the smile had vanished. "He used to take me there when was I was child, only last year the tribal leaders asked him to visit them, alas, that was when his health began to fail him". The Princess fell silent and her eyes glisten as Kingswood could see she was distraught.

"How did you become so good with a pistol?" he enquired quietly. He wanted her to think of something else but he was staggered by her shooting in the heat of battle.

She gave a tiny shrug of her shoulders and tilted her head sideways very slightly. "My father always wanted me to learn about the latest inventions so Diore could be at the fore of the industrialized lands. After the steam powered machines, I also wanted the best arms for our soldiers, so I took it upon myself to learn about the pistols and how to fire them. Become something I quite enjoyed doing, actually". "My father would have preferred that I could use the sword better when I was young. I had the instruction but never really took to it".

Kingswood could see she now looked at the floor with an embarrassed face that he found really endearing. "My father also insisted I had to be good with the sword when I was young" he offered, "I used to hate it, the early morning practice, remembering the drills" he wondered off in thought.

"I hear you are very good" the Princess replied brightly, appearing to appreciate the officers honesty. "That may be down to all the times folk have tried to slay me over the last year!".

#

"Not really the citadel, is it?" observed Lieutenant Pindar in his usual shrill even tone. Sergeant Usk, what do you think?". The short soldier snapped to attention as if they were still in Diore. He gestured at a grunting red faced Karl who was trying to shake the thick bars on their metal cage.

"Bars look solid Lieutenant" grinned Usk, "they are embedded firmly in the cave floor and ceiling. The lock to the door seems well made and would withstand a heavy blow, I would say. Even if we could escape the cage and the four guards, there are only two ways out. One leads out the way we came in, we would never get through that door. The other seems to be through that smaller wooden door on the far side of the cave and I can only hear howling, on the other side, big dogs by the sound of it".

"Very good Sergeant, Sergeant Hawks, what do you think?".

"I think it is too cramp here sir, no air, I will go mad here".

"I meant about escape, I –".

"You need not worry about escape, you Diore filth will not last long here!!" came a deep threatening voice behind them. The men all turned to see two cages away stood a big, brute of a man, with long oily hair covering his wide hairy chest and a fresh slender jagged scar snaking unpleasantly down the side of his face. He grabbed the bars of his cage tightly and shook them violently as he snarled loudly. "I am Sulla the skull splitter, I am wanted for countless slayings in Juno".

There was silence from the soldiers, then Lieutenant Pindar spoke in a befuddled smirking tone.

"So, you escaped from there, to be imprisoned, here?, oh, that is good!!". The other soldiers nearly fell to the floor laughing which only enraged Sulla even more. "YOU LAUGH AT ME?? He screamed, I WILL HAVE MY TEN VICTORIES AND I HOPE YOU THREE ARE AMONG THEM".

"There are four of us you halfwit" exclaimed Pindar who waved his hand casually to one side to dismiss the intrusion and turned his back to face the other soldiers. Sulla roared with anger at this slight and wrestled hard with the bars, only for a hard faced guard to walk over and strike his cage with a rough, heavy looking wooden club."WAIT, - FOR ARENA" he snarled loudly in broken tongue, his face etched with thought at picking the right words. This helped to calm tempers and gave Ben a chance to glance around the cave. The long cave was about twenty paces wide and well lit with oil lanterns that looked strange in their medieval surroundings. Straining his eyes, he could see the walls were rough and uneven but were made by hand, the chiselled marks were unmistakable.

He could see two men, short and skinny were cowering in the corner of Sulla's cage, their faces white with fright. In the cage next to theirs, there were three warrior tribesmen, they were in deep conversation and seemed to be unbothered by their noisy neighbour but would time from time peer to the far end of the cave. They looked like the warriors he had fought in the battle, their bodies looked as solid as rock and the faces were assured, even their eyes showed no weakness. The one in the middle looked very formidable, his head nearly touched the ceiling of the cave such was his height. He reminded Ben of a big mastiff dog who would become a hideous apparition when the need arose. Behind them was another two cages side by side, the men there all had the appearance of confident, battle hardened men whom he witnessed the likes of before. The last cage right at the back only had one guest in it. This one was dressed like the other warrior tribesmen but smaller in stature. He had a black unkept beard that matched his long scruffy heap of hair on his head. He sat strangely, on the floor cross legged staring at the wall, his palms resting on his knees."It will not be easy for someone to fight their way through this mob" he thought out loud.

Time passed slowly and other smaller tribesmen came and went with wooden trays stacked with food and water. Another came with fresh bandages and the guardsman was surprised to see the wise looking elder man take great care with a man who was there when they arrived. He must have suffered a wound to his arm in his last fight. It was clear the man had great skill and even gave the wounded man some herbs for his discomfort and made sure he had plenty of water. Ben could also see some of the other men observing where the man had been wounded and if it made him move differently.

A short while later the captured soldiers talked softly about what may happen. "You should not have taunted Darius" Usk said gravely. "He will want to single you out as a warning to others".

"You are right" agreed the guardsman bitterly, "I did not think, I wonder how angry he was?." At that moment the men could hear music drifting into the cave and the two guards beckoned Ben from his cage. The other two unlocked Sulla's cage and he sprang out like a hungry wolf. His black evil eyes widened as he saw Ben and laughed grotesquely as he drew his thumb slowly across his throat.

"I think Darius was very angry" Lieutenant Pindar observed unsmilingly.

As the two men were escorted through the heavy twin doors, a wall of jeering hit them as they walked out onto the now brightly lit arena. There were crowds of people gathered along one side of the arena, Ben could not make out their faces but it was evident that many were drunk. The music he heard earlier was coming from a band of musicians sitting in an iron gantry bolted to the cavern wall over the heads of the crowd. As well as a vast array of flaming torches placed around the cavern he now looked up to see a huge iron chandler filled with giant blood red candles hanging over the arena. He was so entranced by the incredible noise and the cruel splendour of what he could see. He was abruptly snapped out of it when a booming familiar voice cut through the din like an axe.

Darius himself was now standing above the wooden ladder, wearing a dazzling gold tunic, he held his arms up, the candlelight shone off his numerous jewel encrusted gold rings adorning his fat stubby fingers and the crowds slowly fell silent. "WELCOME" he bellowed across the cavern. "A GLORIOUS WELCOME TO OUR DARING AND BELOVED GUESTS TO THE UNDERWORLD OF IO !". Darius paused as he turned around in a circle to see the cheering crowd, his big gloating smile once again cut through his flabby face as he fed on the applause of his audience. "WE HAVE THE FOULEST, MOST CURSED, WARRIORS EVER TO WALK THE FACE OF THIS WORLD, FIGHTING TO THE DEATH, FOR YOUR BELOVED AMUSEMENT, AS WELL AS FOR THE ODD WAGER", he paused dramatically and the crowds laughed heartily as he gave a long cheeky wink. Ben could see this man was a master at his art in front of an audience and the drunken cheering mob was now deafening. Again he raised his arms and the noise died away, "BUT MY FRIENDS, AS YOU KNOW, MANKIND HAS AWAYS FEARED TO TREAD NEAR THE GATEWAY OF THE UNDERWORLD, FOR FEAR OF THE DIABOLICAL BEASTS THAT LURK HERE!!". At that moment bright orange plumes of flames streaked from the sides across the arena as if an ancient dragon hidden from view had breathed them. Darius pointed to the far end of the arena that had been in pitched darkness, it suddenly became bathed in bright light and Ben could see two men and a woman trapped inside a large wrought iron cage on wheels. They did not look like warriors, the men looked tired and thin. The brown haired woman looked beautiful as she wore what looked like two strips of fur covering her chest and waist, but gave a strange snarl at the crowd as she leant against the bars of her prison. Ben strained his eyes in the unnatural light and looked harder in disbelief as their eyes seemed to be glowing red.

There was a great gasp from the onlookers as well, then the cage disappeared in total darkness, only to reappear some moments later. Now the guardsman jolted backwards in surprise as the cage was once more bathed in light but there were no sign of the three figures. Now there were three wolf- like beasts snapping furiously at the iron bars. Sharp, dagger like teeth jutted from their blunt dark muzzles. Their massive, heavy heads, punctured by glowering red eyes, adorned by large sharp pointed ears sat on top of a wide chest covered in short, coarse stripped fur. With short hind legs and thin longer forelimbs, the creatures did not look like any earthly beast Ben had seen before. Darius spoke again and broke the audience from their trance. "BEHOLD, I PRESENT TO YOU, THE JINN!!, THE SPIRITS OF MISFORTUNE WHO ROAM OUR LANDS AT NIGHT, WHO NOW APPEAR TO YOU AS INCARNATIONS OF THESE MONSTERS. ONE BITE WILL SHATTER A MANS ARM!, FROM A DEVIL THAT HAS NEVER BEEN CONQURED." Darius now glanced wickedly at Ben as the guards brought the two men to the centre of the arena. "MY HUMBLE GUESTS YOU HAVE ENTERED THE UNDERWORLD OF IO, NOW MEET IT's

DENIZENS". Again the crowd cheered and waved feverishly. "IN OUR FIRST CONTEST TONIGHT WE HAVE TWO DESPARATE SOULS WHO WILL DO ANYTHING FOR THEIR FREEDOM AND A FORTUNE!."

Ben who was now exchanging stares with Sulla as they faced each other, was irritated by the incessant blabbering.

"Why don's you take one step forward and fall off the edge, I will give you a glorious Underworld welcome, you fat slug!".

"EVEN THE DARKEST GAOL COULD NOT HOLD THIS MAN!. FRESH FROM HIS FIRST VICTORY HERE, I PRESENT TO YOU, SULLA THE SKULL CRUSHER!!!. Sulla roared savagely at the mention of his name but kept staring at Ben the whole time.

Darius now wore an ugly smirking face. "NOW, TO SHOW YOU GOOD PEOPLE THAT WE SCOUR THE LANDS FOR- DIFFERENT MEN FOLK,- FROM EASTERN MIMAS BUT WITHOUT HIS MOUNT TO ADVISE HIM, WE HAVE THE GUARDSMAN!".

Now the men from the crowd were pointing at Ben laughing, mock neighing noises drifted around the arena and unflattering curses were screamed at him. Ben could feel his hands tremble and felt a knot of fear in his stomach. He now took slow breaths and cleared his mind for the task ahead. He knew he must not let anger become a mist in the battle, but get his opponent vexed instead. Now the guards had placed his two swords in front of him on the cavern floor. A long heavy wooden club with strips of iron wrapped around a rounded end was placed down in front of Sulla.

"That is a nice back scratcher you have there" he goaded, "Did you get that from your Mother, when she gave you that scar?" he asked with a broad grin. As Darius finished,

"LET THE CONTEST BEGAN, Sulla sprinted at the guardsman with a animal like bellow, he snatched up his club as he passed and span around to flay Ben, only to hit air. Gathering his swords, the guardsman had dived down, rolled up from the ground and lunged forward to his left. His left hand sliced down Sulla's ribs with the straight sword, causing his opponent to grimace in pain as the big man swung the back of his claw like hand across Ben's face. The force of the blow turned his head sideways but he instinctively turned around in the same direction and landed a heavy kick to Sulla's leading leg as he knocked the massive club to one side with both his swords. Sulla, loudly screaming a foul curse he stumbled backwards onto the floor as the blade of a dull curved sword barely missed his throat. Clearly rattled by the move and in great pain, Sulla swiftly got to his feet then stumbled down once again, desperately keeping his distance from the guardsman as he grimly held onto his club. Keen to keep the advantage Ben advanced swiftly at his opponent, only for a burst of orange flames to spew at him from the side of the arena. He jumped to his right but still felt a searing pain on his left shoulder, as he clattered to the floor heavily, he rubbed his eyes furiously as tears poured from them. Half seeing, half hearing his heavy adversary now painfully grunting after him, he jumped back as the heavy club narrowly missed his knee and thudded down on the stone floor. Tears still streaming down his cheeks he managed to cross his swords above his head to block a mighty downward blow. With a grunt he tried to shrug the club away from it's owner, only for Sulla to crash his forehead viciously into Ben's face, sending him sprawling to the floor. He now fumbled madly for his swords as Sulla charged at him like a crazed bull.

"I WILL SEE YOU SCORCHING IN HELL, MIMAS WEAKLING!" he cursed as he heaved his weapon above his head to deliver the mortal strike. With a grunt of pain and a flash of movement, Ben slid up on one knee and drove his straight guardsman sword into his attackers belly. He left the sword in his mortally wounded foe as he sprang to both feet and stepped behind Sulla. Holding the handle of his curved sword firmly with both hands, he brought it down across the murderers back. Sulla's shriek pierced the din, his heavy club slipped from his hands as his big legs buckled and he crashed face first on the cold arena floor. Ben stood ready but the man did not move.

"You go first, I will follow later" he panted.

His eyes were still on the fallen Sulla when Darius's voice silenced the crowd once again. "WHAT A SURPRISE VICTORY MY FRIENDS, BUT AS WE SAY HERE IN THE UNDERWORLD OF IO, WHO KNOWS WHO THE GHASTLY HAND OF DEATH WILL TOUCH NEXT!". He said the last few words more slowly and Ben could hear some members of the crowd shouting the same words with much merriment. Darius voice sounded the same but as the guards gently took his swords and led him back, he could see that the gaze of the host was still on him.

CHAPTER FIVE

THE LION OF THE UNDERWORLD

"He did it!" cried Usk as Ben was brought back in. Still holding a blood soaked rag to his nose and holding his left arm close to his body, he gave a little grin.

"Inside" said one of the burly guards as he unlocked the cage door and opened it, "The healer comes, - make you feel-better ". Ben nodded and walked in as the cage door slammed behind him.

"You did not expect me to return?" he asked with a mischievous smile.

"I did but Karl owes me two flagons of ale" Usk replied in a wounded tone.

Karl shrugged his shoulders meekly, "glad you are alive though, sergeant". The men laughed and patted the guardsman on the shoulder much to his agony. The old frail looking healer man appeared with a bucket of cold water, some rags and a small glass bottle of foul smelling ointment. He instantly began to work on the burnt shoulder as Ben enthralled his comrades with the tale of the contest.

Two of the skinny men who were in Sulla's cage were called up and they had to be dragged out by the giggling guards. Both looked petrified and one even sobbed uncontrollably. The warriors could hear an eerie chattering laugh from the arena that even seemed to subdue the crowd. Moments later they could hear the bloodthirsty crowd once again but the door remained closed. The cave was then plunged into silence as the tribesman at the back of the cave was escorted from his cage.

His face showed nothing as he calmly walked past the other cages. The other warriors respectfully nodded but the other three tribesmen shouted at him in their own tongue and the biggest struck one of his cage bars so hard with his elbow, the bar bent like straw. One of the confident battle hardened warriors was also called out and needed no encouragement. Though not big, his body appeared lean and fit and his dark brown eyes bulged with excitement at his new opponent. He rubbed his right hand over his shaven brown hair and started bouncing on the soles of his feet at the anticipation of the forth coming fight. The man seemed hardly concerned by this aggressive gesture and casually kept looking forward as he was led out to the din of the bloodthirsty mob. Lieutenant Pindar was now instructing his men in earnest and gleaned as much knowledge as he could from the guardsmans experience.

"This fire" he said thoughtfully rubbing his jaw,

We are not in a volcano" he continued looking at the three soldiers in turn, "and I do not believe it to be the work of unnatural beasts, demons or even the Tooth Fairy!". "Manmade, I would gamble!, hidden fire pits perhaps, the fire fanned by giant air bellows", that is how I would do it" he reasoned out loud.

"I think I have seen Great sergeant Task breathe fire before" said Usk with a cheeky grin. All the men laughed hard at this one.

"So best we try to keep to the centre of the arena, is that what you are saying Hawks" enquired the Lieutenant respectfully to get every ones attention once more.

"I think so Sir, the arena is well lit but the best place to be seen by all the paying crowd would be right in the middle" he said with distaste. "Also" he added as an afterthought, "I was winning at the time, not sure if this happens in the arena to alter the balance of a contest sometimes".

"Perhaps", Pindar said carefully, reading Ben's eyes, "So be prepared for anything men and Sergeant Hawks,

- it is clear you a good soldier, try not to anger Darius again". Ben took the advice and meekly nodded that he understood. At that moment the goal door swung open and the tribesmen walked back in. As before, the man looked unfazed and was breathing as if he had been on a short morning stroll. Ben stared at the man to discover any clues about him, the short warrior glanced back with his striking green eyes and showed a mild curious expression, then looked back in the direction he was walking as the guards locked him securely in his cage.

Next sergeant Usk was called out, his jesting manner had now vanished and he appeared serious and his eyes shone with determination. The other soldiers patted his back and gave him encouragement as walked out with another of the battle hardened fighters.

The heavy door slammed shut after them, Pindar could see the guardsman was vexed and was swift to put him at ease. "He talks a lot, -well constantly" amended the officer with a thought, "different beast in a fight though, I have seen him slay three outlaws single handed. He will prevail".

Right enough, it seemed only moments later that Usk was escorted back, beads of sweat poured of his shiny bald head but he was back to his happy self. "Talked him to death!" he winked, showing off a black eye but otherwise seemed unscathed. Karl followed next and again came back victorious. He did not fare so well, with blood dripping from cuts above his left eye, right shoulder and back, Lieutenant Pindar called for the healer right away.

"He, - comes" replied one of the guards, "Now, your turn, to fight" he ordered loudly as he stepped to one side so the officer could leave the cage.

"Easy victory" exclaimed Usk, "won the last tournament in Diore".

"Task never bothers to enter" Pindar laughed as he slapped Ben on the back as he left the cage and looked to see who he would be fighting. A huge shadow passed over him as the biggest tribesmen warrior stood there wearing a cruel smile. He laughed deeply to the ceiling and walked stoically to the arena, the guards would not go near him. The soldiers exchanged glances and Ben looked around to take his mind off the contest. He could see the short tribesmen warrior at the back of the cave, staring in the direction of the door, then looked at Ben. He gave a short solemn shake of his head and turned away. Ben and Usk busied themselves helping Karl to make sure he was comfortable and that his pain was easing. Karl would normally have told them to leave him in peace but he realised they were over doing it to take their mind of the Lieutenant's plight. They had ran out of things to do and Usk was describing his previous victory when they could hear the din of the cheering crowd sweep into the gaol. Even Karl joined his comrades with a yelp of pain at the bars of the cage. The three men peered out to see the victorious officer, only to watch the warrior tribesmen walk up to their cage.

"Good, - contest" he said, panting slightly, his eyes were full of excitement, he then turned to face the four vexed looking guards, he bellowed in his native tongue and pointed to the unkempt fighter at the back. Plucking an empty wooden bucket from the floor he hurled it with such force that it flew across the length of the cave and smashed into wooden slithers as it hit the last cage.

The inhabitant of the cage stood his ground but turned his head away as bits of the bucket bounced of his chest. The powerful man pushed a shouting guard to the floor as if he was a child, then walked slowly to his own cage, still giving the unkept man a withering stare.

As the biggest guard swiftly locked the door, Usk gave the nearest cage bar a hard thud with the palm of his hand."THIS PLACE" he spat loudly, "will be the death of us all" he finished quietly still looking towards the arena.

"He was a fine blade, what chance do we have?" moaned Karl.

"He said he always wanted to die on the battlefield, if he had a choice" observed Usk grimly.

"That is what this place is, a battlefield and we must treat it as such" spoke the guardsman as he stared towards the doors to the arena. "As long as you have breath in your body, you always have a chance" Ben offered with a strained smile. "Lieutenant Pindar would not want you to give up, we have a duty-".

"Do not speak as if you knew the Lieutenant, the other sergeant rasped, "nor remind us of our duty. The Princess may have escaped but we were defeated and this hell is our sentence!".Usk slumped down in the corner, his face in his hands. The guardsman tried to speak, then stopped thinking that everyone needed some rest.

After a long strange silence, the cave went quiet as everyone tried to sleep and gather much needed rest.

After a long sleep, Ben woke up feeling sore and stiff. The other soldiers were still asleep but there was a low murmur of voices as the other men began to stir. Thinking it would be good to give Usk and Karl some time to mourn their Lieutenant, he waved over to the guards to signal if he could stretch his legs. When he had first seen that the fighters were allowed to do this, he could not believe his eyes but really he could see it made good sense. There were deep lines scratched into the stone ground around each of the cages. They were about two paces from the cage bars and the men were shown a cat O, nine tails when they were shown their cages. "FOOT, - OVER LINE, EAT THIS !" cried the biggest guard nursing the whip, the men understood right away.

Leaving the cage, even for a short time, seemed priceless. His shoulder was covered in red blisters and welts but the swelling grew less thanks to the healer. The other warriors stayed in their cages whispering to each other and glanced nervously at the tall tribesmen from time to time. He snarled a curse as Ben passed by, "What's that you said?, good victory?, very good of you" he muttered in a cheerless voice. Some of the other fighters nodded with respect as he passed their cages. He strolled over to the thick wooden door at the back of the gaol. He could hear the strange chattering laugh again, coming from the other side and it chilled his blood. "What are those infernal beasts!" he cried out loud.

"Desert Hyenas but they never brought them through here" came a softly spoken voice behind him. Ben whirled round to see the long dark haired tribesmen sitting cross legged on his cage floor, lost in thought.

"Normally they leave man alone but I have heard the guards say that they are only fed live prisoners and are taunted by Darius himself to make them vicious". The man looked at the guardsman as he spoke but not in an intimidating way, there was curiosity in his eyes.

"Darius" said Ben with a dry smile, "not really- a pleasant man is he?". "My name – is Sergeant guardsman- Hawks!", he stood tall as he raised his voice.

"Why do your people talk loudly to us as if that will make you easier to understand?" enquired the man with a bemused smile. Ben's cheeks flushed pink as he realised what he did. "You are right about Darius. I am known here as the Lion of the Underworld" the man said quietly.

"Did not get on with your family?" Ben asked with a mischievous grin.

The Lion's face bulged with merriment and stroked his mane like beard as he gave a small snort of laughter. "I have not been in the mood for merriment for some time. I would like to share my real name but I fear you would not survive the night".

"Hmm, think you may be right" Ben whispered as he could see one of the guards was now staring at them as they spoke.

Then a thought struck him. "You talked of the hyenas,- they are not these, - Jinn then?, he asked slightly afraid.

The Lion gave another snort of laughter, "No sergeant, that is only a story for children and travellers who would believe-" he stopped abruptly, "please excuse me, I did not mean to offend".

"Never got offended and you speak my tongue better than I". "My Father always taught me to honour our own traditions but learn and respect the customs of others", the man explained. I also have travelled vast distances across the real desert with the merchants, it is said a wise man never stops learning".

The Lion then licked his lips, "could I trouble you for some water?, my flask is over there", he pointed next to his cage.

Ben picked up the large leather flask but a familiar smell filled his nostrils. "Are you ill or wounded?" he asked in surprise.

"NO" the Lion looked around to see who was listening and threw a dangerous glance at the guards. "Why do you ask?" his green eyes were alert and interested. "A friend I met last year taught me about the herbs used in medicine. This water smells like a herb they use to make a man drowsy ours is plain water. Ben stopped and the two men looked at each other. The Lion cursed in his native tongue but some noise at the other end of the gaol made Ben turn around. Usk was making ungentlemanly gestures at the big tribesmen warrior who looked none too happy and appeared ready to remove his cage door with his bare hands.

Taking his chance while the guards were busy, he threw the tainted water away and swiftly filled the flask up from another nearby cask. "Thank you sergeant" gasped the Lion as he was handed the water.

"You are welcome, best get back to my cage now, though".

"Wait!, you have helped me, I must honour my debt. The tall warrior is known as Aaryan the Strong, let not his size fool you, he may be as strong as an ox but his blade is more skilful than most. He is not like the rest of the tribesmen, he enjoys killing and is vengeful!. That is a deadly brew, baiting this man will only make harder to defeat". "His eyes now looked into the guardsman with heartfelt sorrow, "you are the only man they have allowed to speak to me, I do not think they intend for you to leave here,- ever".

As he got back to his cage, things had calmed down. The other tribesmen were talking to Aaryan the Strong in a bid to quell his temper and this seemed to work to the relief of the concerned guards.

As the cage door was locked behind him, Ben could see that Usk was looking pleased with himself. "Thought you may want to talk to that stranger" he grinned, "caused a distraction to give you time".

The guardsman inhaled sharply. "That was good of you sergeant but that man is beyond dangerous." "He wants to kill me anyway" said Usk mournfully, "I will not make it easy for him," he said staring at the crazed figure.

Ben sat down and told the soldiers what the Lion had said about Aaryan, them leaving the Underworld and the tainted water. "Makes sense", offered Usk who was back to his gleeful self, "it sounds to me that Darius does not want that man to go anywhere either". Ben nodded and looked around carefully and spoke in a hushed voice. "We need to escape, we cannot stay here, escape is our only chance". "How!", Usk asked with a look of exasperation. "If we got free from our cage and got past the guards, there is still those massive doors to the arena and they only open from the outside".

"Who knows what is outside waiting for us, could even be those Jinn" added Karl. "They are myths, they are not real Karl" replied the guardsman now feeling very weary.

"They can turn into myths as well!" he asked in surprise, looking at each man in turn.

Ben blinked in disbelief, "honestly Karl?".

"The door to the back of the cave is a way out, I think", he said, mostly trying to convinced himself. "Where the howling comes from??, that is a serious gamble" stated Usk looking very flustered.

"The myths may be there as well" muttered Karl crossing his arms in fear.

"Oh, That is it!," snapped Ben "I want to go in that cage with him" he said nodding at Aaryan.

CHAPTER SIX

THE OLD ALLIANCE

#

Kingswood's thigh was feeling much better, abeit his wound still ached when he moved. Nevertheless at mid day he was at the training courtyard, the cold breeze made him cough but it felt clean and refreshed him. He was alone and wanted to have his polished sabre in his hand and practice some sword drills but he knew the wound needed time to heal properly.

Looking over the battlements at Io, he racked his mind again and again if there was something he could have done differently, did Ben have to give his life?, he wondered.

On hearing someone clear their throat behind him, he turned to see the formidable figure of great sergeant Task standing to attention five paces behind him. "Lieutenant Kingswood, I have a message from his highness Grand Prince Friedrich". Kingswood instantly gathered his thoughts,

"Yes, Great sergeant?". "Your presence has been requested to a meeting this evening at the Great hall. Formal dress, a servant will come to your chambers to escort you".

"Please tell his Highness, it would be an honour" Kingswood replied weakly, trying to put his doubts to one side. Task bowed sharply, turned to leave, then turned around again. "Anything else Great sergeant?" the officer could not hide his bewilderment.

Task still stood to attention as he spoke. "It is not my place to say Lieutenant but it was not your fault sergeant Hawks did not come back. To fight so well he must have thought the risk was worthwhile. You had to give the order, if you had not, the Princess would not have escaped and matters would be far much darker than they are now!".

The officer gave a small nod as he recognised the sentiment. "Thank you Great sergeant". He turned to look over the battlements again as Task left him alone once more. "How can you repay a debt of gratitude to a dead man?" he wondered out loud.

#

That evening Kingswood found himself outside the tall ebony double doors of the Great hall. Even in his ceremonial tunic he felt scruffy, glancing around the enormous brightly lit hall at the other guests. Feeling out of place and at unease he wondered why he had been invited at all when he felt a soft tap on his shoulder. He stepped forward, turned his head and was delighted to see Princess Marie standing before him. Dressed in a bright red dress shining like a ruby, that held her chest tightly, his words had deserted him. "Lieutenant Kingswood" she cried softly, "you look very, dashing..., oh no, did I just say dashing", she giggled nervously as her cheeks glowed.

"You did" he answered meekly with a strange smile and a small shrug of his shoulders. "Never been called that before, - but dashing is good, I like dashing" he uttered, trying to sound calm but failing completely.

"Can I offer you some wine?. Her eyes sparkled as she took two silver goblets from the tray of a passing serving girl.

The officer took a goblet with thanks, as he muttered under his breath, "dashing is good??, please, somebody stand me in front of a loaded cannon!!".

"Pardon, I did not hear that, this hall can be quite noisy".

"Oh, I said, eh-, please stand by me when we play some backgammon". Both now had red faces and looked around to see who was looking. The Lieutenant gave a slight cough and continued. "I am honoured by the invitation, - though, perhaps daunted by it" he whispered into her ear.

The Princess gave another small laugh and a even bigger smile. "You have nothing to fear here" she said glancing around at the guests. "The citizens of Diore are still a little vexed about the help we have had from Mimas in the past. Though now we must look to the future. Her kind words helped to put the young officer at ease as a short fierce looking grey haired man in bright red uniform walked over to them and snapped to attention. "Ah, Commander Engels, head of Diores Defence, I trust we are ready to start soon, I take it you remember Lieutenant Kingswood?."

"How can I forget!" he barked," we owe you a debt of bravery my dear boy, I fear we will never be able to repay."

"I hope the wound is better?, no doubt it will leave a good scar to show your valour. Never thought the tribesmen were capable of such an act. They will pay dearly for this!!" he hissed bitterly.

"Commander, that is what we are here to discuss" the Princess reminded in a soothing tone.

A small hand bell echoed across the hall and the guests walked to their seats around a long ebony table in the middle. "Please, Marco here will show you to your seat, remember to keep breathing" she said with a knowing look in her eyes.

Kingswood gave a long bow and followed the tall slender servant boy to a exquisitely carved ebony seat at the middle of the table.

Glancing around the table, everyone looked important but also angry and vexed. The white Princess stood up and cleared her throat, the other dignitaries looked up in silence.

"Thank you for breaking away from your important duties", her voice was now firm and assured. "As you are all aware, we stand at a chasm of uncertainty, blunder now" her voice was now shaking, "and our children will look back in sorrow. "Commander of defence, Commander Engels, please tell everyone at the table what steps have been taken so far".

The short grey haired man jumped to his feet, puffed out his chest proudly and seemed more fierce than before. "The Diore Militia are now patrolling our lands, we have all our brave soldiers guarding the whole of the river border of Diore for any sign of danger". "We are also arming as many of our sail barges as possible with cannon post haste". He stopped and gazed around the table, his dark bloodshot eyes looking for approval. "Any attack from the hills will be blasted into dust".

Cheering and clapping erupted from the dignitaries. "That was popular" sighed Kingswood in a concerned fashion.

Another figure stood up, he was short but his belly bulged heavily as if he was with child. His thick heavy gold chain hanging around his fat neck gleamed in the candle light. "Your Highness, honoured guests, as always that was the strong assurance we were expecting from the Commander. On behalf of the merchants of Diore, we would be happy to fund an expedition into Io to force reparations from the tribesmen".

The cheering and clapping was now an ugly din that filled the great hall. "Reparations "groaned Kingswood under his breath. "Because that never fails to demean the lands who must pay. I gather you will lead the way to the bloodbath, you gutless worm...".

"Lieutenant Kingswood". Kingswood frozed, then slowly looked up in horror to see that now everyone was staring in his direction. The rich merchant smiled sickly, "I nearly forgot my place, perhaps our friends in Mimas would wish to honour the old alliance by sending their own army on such a venture".

The man theatrically nodded around the long table. "You conniving, - bastard!!!" thought the officer as a tall, fiery haired man rose up.

"Maurice is right!, let the Protector of Almanthea tell us their plans. With the might of Mimas behind us, we will yield to no one" he boasted loudly.

Kingswood's face was taut and his palms moist. He was afraid of this and the urgent parchment he received by bird this afternoon would only make matters worse. He shakily stood to his feet, bowed deeply to the Princess then took the deepest of breaths. "This afternoon I received an urgent message from Captain Nicolus, as you know he advises the council of Almanthea. He paused to steel himself for the inevitable onslaught. Thirty soldiers will be at camp on the banks of the river Gold by sunset tomorrow. A column of caravans carrying extra supplies of gunpowder and muskets will arrive the same day.

A chorus of disapproval echoed around the table as the obnoxious bald headed merchant stood up again. "Pardon me Lieutenant, - I do not hear so good these days" he addressed the officer but looked at his fellow guests. "Did you say thirty soldiers?", again acting as if he was on a stage.

Kingswood could see the displeasure on the faces of the dignitaries as they muttered loudly to each other. He spoke again slowly, "Off course more soldiers will be despatched if required but with the skirmishes Mimas suffered last year, the council of Almanthea has deemed it, - prudent, - that the regular army continues to watch our borders. Also," he swallowed deeply and carried on."The Captain has the same thoughts as I", he could feel his throat drying up.

"Which are?" asked the fiery haired man who looked like he would not approve of the answer.

"I believe the ambush may be only the work of a small minority" he explained carefully.

"What difference does that make!" sneered Maurice loudly.

"It – means that since I have arrived here, I have tried to seek out the truths, rather than common folklore in an attempt to avoid a war. The desert tribes of Io wish only to live peacefully with their own ways and beliefs. However, although they may disagree with each other, they are honour bound to unite, to drive any invader from their lands" he said at the pompous fool.

"I did not know that cowardice was so rife in Mimas" snarled the fiery haired man in anger. Kingswood drew breath to defend his honour when a croaking, gravel like voice silenced the gathering.

"In all my years at this table I have never witnessed a honoured guest insulted so". Kingswood turned to see the elderly silver maned man standing weakly at the other end of the table.

"But – your Highness, his feeble gesture dishonours you-".

"Dishonours !!" cried Grand Prince Friedrich as he banged both his hands on the hard table. "This man was wounded and his sergeant slain in battle with our brave loyal men so my beloved daughter could escape. A fighter like you should see that, Dorian!".

The man looked like he suffered a blow to his face as he bowed low to the Prince and turned to the Lieutenant. "Forgive me Lieutenant Kingswood", Dorian growled softly, his eyes fixed on the floor. "Those were dumb words I used". Kingswood respectfully nodded his acceptance as Maurice whined on. "This is all very well your highness but how can the Lieutenant prove that not all the tribes are behind these fiendish acts".

Again all eyes fell on the young officer. Thoughts and emotions whirred around his head as he blurted out, "Because I will go and see for myself!".

"That would be a wasted life!, do not tempt fate after my foolish words" Dorian pleaded sincerely.

"It is the only way, your Great sergeant Task has informed me that the tribesmen have always respected the safe passage of an emissary through their lands. I will deliver a truthful message of hope to the tribal leader and keep my eyes and ears open. With the blessing of Diore, I shall ride at first light tomorrow".

There was now a deathly silence hanging around the table but the ageing Grand Prince spoke first. "You risk too much, young Lieutenant", the elderly man said with a resigned expression. "You have our blessing and I hope fate looks kindly upon you and your brave actions".

There was now loud clapping as the dignitaries stood up and applauded, some even cheered. His heart felt a little warmer with this response and smiled slightly as he glanced at the Princess, who starred at him, her face a mask of pity and sorrow.

#

Time passed swiftly and the warriors were warned that more contests would start shortly. Again, Ben was called out first but was struck with fear as he was led out by himself. "Must be the hyenas", he cried out loud to himself in horror. He racked his mind when he hunted, to think of useful ploys against wild beasts. The guards left him in the middle of the arena, as the crowd jeered loudly with the same horse sounds and tauts as before.

He stared up at Darius but was staggered by his hosts look of supreme confidence. He looked in the direction of where the big iron cage was wheeled out but nothing came. Suddenly bursts of flame spat out from the sides and in between them strolled out a tall pale faced man, dressed in black trousers and sleeveless tunic. His deep yellow hair was only matched in brightness by his piercing cold blue eyes. He stepped slowly, laughing and waving to the crowd and stopped three paces away from a finely polished sabre on the arena floor. Ben could not believe how lavish the handle looked, the pommel was pure white and the cross guard consisted of strands of metal that looked as if it was made by an artist. The man looked up at Darius and gave a short bow and then turned to face his opponent.

An evil sneer cut across his young face as he looked at the guardsman from his boots, up to his vexed face. "I CAN ACTUALLY SEE THE GHASTLY HAND OF DEATH ALREADY TAPPING ON HIS SHOULDER!", he shouted to the crowd, gleefully.

Ben returned his look, the man did not look big or threatening but something troubled deep inside him, this man was not all he seemed.

Darius introduced Ben as insulting as before, then introduced the dark stranger to the crowd.

"ONCE AGAIN, WE HAVE AN OLD FAVOURITE AT THE UNDERWORLD. HE COMES WHEN SUMMONED LIKE A TRUE DEMON, HE SLAYS HIS VICTIMS, THEN RETURNS TO THE LADIES OF THE NIGHT!". After this remark, Darius paused as he glanced around the crowd and was rewarded by a chorus of laughter and applause. "FROM DEIMOS ITSELF, ONE OF THEIR VERY OWN MASTER SWORDSMEN, I PRESENT, TIBERIUS THE TORMENTOR!!".

The crowd cheered even harder, as Tiberius walked up to his fellow warrior with his left hand outstretched ,

Ben feeling a trap, shook his head and stepped back. This brought a burst of laughter from the yellow haired man. "HE WILL NOT ACCEPT MY HAND" he teased, "SO I WILL TAKE HIS HEAD!!!" he roared to the crowd who jeered so loud at Ben the din was deafening.

Darius was clearly enjoying the commotion as he boomed "LET THE CONTEST BEGIN!". Both men were at their weapons in a blink of an eye but as Ben grasped both his swords he barely had time to angle his body as a polished blade darted past his shoulder. The man dashed past but he swung his right hand around to reveal a stiletto that sliced the lobe of Ben's right ear.

Stepping back, he cursed in pain. "Did you become a sergeant with a roll of the dice?" goaded his opponent with a gloating laugh.

"You wish to talk me to death?" snarled the guardsman as he circled his adversary warily. "Methinks, that is your true skill".

The man in black let out a sneering chuckle as he stood sideways on to Ben in a classical swordsman stance. "Oh, you will soon see my true skill, my horse loving friend". Ben steeled himself to attack only for his foe to shuffle forward and attack with a darting lunge. Again such was the swiftness, he could not parry the strike but recoiled his body away from the approaching blade like a startled cat. This time the sabre slashed his chest and he yelped out in frustrated pain, swallowing hard, the guardsman now charged forward. Tiberius now shuffled backwards without a care, parrying a thrusting blow, then ducked his head as Ben's curved sword missed as well.

The yellow haired man was about to speak when Ben's left boot lashed into his thigh and sent him stumbling back several paces. "Not too bad" he praised softly,

I now have two worthy opponents to best, I will have earned my reward this time" he grinned, as he lightly dusted off the boot print from his garment.

At that moment, something glistened, hanging from his neck, it was shaped like a hunting bird. "Nice trinket you have there" remarked Ben loudly. "Who did you stab in the back for that piece of fools treasure?".

"Your mother" snapped back Tiberius gleefully, his light eyebrows dancing in tandem, he was clearly enjoying the war of words. With no warning in his eyes, he advanced forward at the same moment as Ben realised he was backing away from the middle of the arena. The guardsman sprang to his right as two tongues of flame hissed out, singed his opponents backside and caused him to skip up in the air and scream in agony.

Recovering his wits, he saw Tiberius had stood still, pawing at his eyes with his right hand. Keen to gain the advantage, Ben ran with all his breath He plunged his straight sword at the heart of Tiberius and when the

Tormentor barely parried his blade, he whipped his curved sword in a deep upward arc. Feigning his discomfort, his adversary tilted his head away from the incoming strike, then rammed the white ivory pommel of his sabre hard into Ben's face. Failing backwards onto the hard arena floor, Ben rolled away from his opponent still clutching his swords. Tears were pouring from his eyes as he wiped his sleeve across his nose to stem the flowing blood.

He was still kneeling down as he carefully watched Tiberius smirking, as the swordsman strolled around the middle of the arena. "I watched that Lieutenant you arrived with, fight Aaryan, now you can meet him!!" he sneered callously. Rage erupted inside the guardsman and forgetting his training, he scrambled to his feet and threw his guardmans sword at the Tormentors chest. Surprised, the slender man maintained his pose and turned and whipped his body away to one side as the heavy missile narrowly soared past. "You are good but did you mean to do this?" Tiberius said smirking, he threw his stiletto up in the air, caught the tip of the blade and stepped forward as the shiny blade darted through the air and landed in Ben's left shoulder.

Squealing in searing pain, slumping onto one knee, the guardsman gritted his teeth and plucked the stiletto out and flung it across the arena floor as Tiberius ran at him for the final onslaught. Ben once again jumped up but more shakily this time and turned sideways as he parried his foe's thrust. Swords still touching, the two men wrestled with all their strength until Tiberius stepped past Ben and forced both blades around in an arc and then crashing to the floor. Planting his foot on the dull curved sword, pinning it down, he sneered viciously, "You know, when that dandy was slain, he made a horrible din!".

Frantically fumbling at the hilt of his Trapped sword, Ben stood upright as the small curved knife burst upwards and slashed across the throat of his assailant. Staggering backwards, he dropped his sabre, Tiberius gurgled uncontrollably, as his hands clutched his throat, his eyes wide with fear and disbelief.

"Ben's voice was slow and short of breath. "Did he make – a din like that?".

His face now ashen, the stricken Tormentor took several laboured steps forward, falling to his knees, he reached out his left bloodied hand, as if to grab his out of reach foe. His blue eyes burning with hatred, "Mimas filth!" he spat as his face because lifeless and he collapsed onto the floor.

"Eastern, Mimas filth" Ben corrected, still panting, his nose still dripping blood, he gazed around the arena.

There was a stunned silence as if nobody had realised the contest had finished, one man started clapping in appreciation of a worthy battle, then others followed until the Underworld was full of respectful applause and cheering. Still on unsteady feet but exhausted, he gazed around the cavern until Darius caught his eye. The man looked at him darkly and he knew he was still in grave danger. "THE GUARDSMAN IS VICTORIOUS ONCE MORE" he declared loudly over the cheering with a greatly forced smile. He then gave a nasty stare to the guards in the arena and nodded sharply to the gaol.

Back in his cage Usk and Karl eagerly asked about the fight, once the healer had cast his spell once more."So he had a good sword arm, knew how to unsettle a seasoned soldier and talked about rewards, in a contest?" said the other sergeant trying to reason things out in his head.

"He was better than good!, he is still inside my head now. Were it not for the hidden dagger, I would be the one lying on his face out there!".

"You say he had a silver amulet of a falcon around his neck?, are you certain it was a falcon".

"It was a hunting bird, I could see it had a hooked beak and looked like a falcon when it dives onto it's prey", Ben gave Usk an look of exasperation. "He was trying to stick me with his sabre, what difference does it make??".

Usk was still grinning as he put his palm up to explain. "I have seen a officer from Deimos wear a silver amulet of an eagle when he came to Diore last year. Everyone treated the man with a fearful respect and some soldiers would not even look in his direction. Great sergeant Task told me that only an officer in the Charonese army, that had trained and won a tournament in Deimos, could wear such an amulet.

The men sat on the stone floor looking vexed. "Who else do they have here?" cried Usk in desperation. While they slept, some more men had been brought in to make up for the slain. One such warrior limped back from his contest as Usk had lost his usual jovial grin. "I feel alright but Karl can hardly walk" he whispered.

It was as if the guards had heard as one came over to their cage. "You two,- rest!- no fight tonight", he commanded.

"Lucky me" exaled Ben spitefully as he wrestled with a piece of herb covered cloth plugging his nose.

When the guards called out the next pair, a deathly silence fell around the cages. The Lion walked slowly from his cage as Aaryan the Strong wrenched his cage door open, bellowing like an enraged bear, he pushed past all four guards, kicked one of the bars in from Ben's cage and stormed towards the door to the arena without giving his opponent a second glance.

"Well at least there is one man Darius despises more than you" Usk stated without smiling. The guardsman had shuffled over to the bars.

"For your own sake, keep moving around" he urged the Lion as he passed their cage. The man gave a small nod but looked very much like a soldier marching off to a war!".

Time passed slowly and some of the warriors had murmured about how long the contest had lasted. Everyone in the gaol listened intently but could only hear the din from the mindless mob. "You think you can best Aaryan the Strong?" sergeant Usk enquired hopefully.

"I sincerely do not know if I could best either of them" replied the guardsman honestly whose eyes were still on the heavy wooden arena doors.

"But you fight with two swords. Is that what they teach you in Jovia?" asked Karl in a befuddled voice.

"No".

"That tribesmen bow you carry, - do all the guardsmen in Eastern Mimas carry a.."

"No".

"Why do they call you the horse talkers for?, is it because...".

Ben was about to roar "NO!!" to Karl, when the gaol doors opened. All three men turned to see which warrior had survived the contest. Jubilation surged through Ben's body as he saw the Lion limped towards them. One side of his face was badly bruised, he gripped his left side, grimacing as he walked. He returned Ben's smile as he passed but the whole cave could see he was in great pain.

"Well, his ill fortune is our good fortune" remarked Usk quietly. "Well, one of us may have to face him next" he added defensively when he saw the surprised faces on his companions.

CHAPTER SEVEN
THE EMISSARY

Dawn, the next day, Kingswood lead his mount from the Citadel. He wanted to stretch his legs before he started the daunting journey. The bright yellow sheen was now touching the tiled roof tops of the town and the chorus of enthusiastic bird song filled the morning air.

Once on his mount, he soon reached the river moorings to see a dark stout figure proudly standing to attention "Lieutenant Kingswood, Grand Prince Friedrich asked me to make sure you had everything needed for such a journey" he enquired respectfully.

"A thousand armed soldiers and a fleet of cannon barges would be helpful" the Lieutenant replied meekly.

A big grin spread across Task's face, "Our best Protection would be travelling under the shield of an Emissary.

"Our best protection?", the officer raised an eyebrow as he dismounted.

"I know the lands and some of the customs, for when I used to escort the Grand Price himself, I am at your service, our barge awaits".

Although wide, the clear blue river was calm, there was not a cloud in the sky and the fresh cool breeze made Kingswood feel quite relaxed. He nearly had to remind himself of where he was heading and the dangers he may face.

They slowly disembarked with their mounts as soon as they reached the other side.

A group of curious fisherman came over to bid the strangers good day and were quite personable and courteous, then Task tapped the officer on the shoulder. As Kingswood turned he could see two tribal warriors standing several paces away. Like the other warriors they seen before, the two looked strong and proud, they were dressed in flowing white robes but they seemed curious rather than threatening. Task swiftly uttered some words in their own tongue while keeping their gaze. When Kingswood heard the word "Emissary", the two warriors glanced over at Kingswood, nodded respectfully and carried on speaking with Task.

Kingswood looked around at the fisherman who had now set sail in their boat and were merrily getting their nets ready to fish. The air was cool and the land appeared quite idyllic, very different than a few days ago he reminded himself. "Only man can make a battlefield in a paradise" he observed out loud with a shake of his head.

"Lieutenant Kingswood" called Task politely and firmly. The officer shook himself from his pleasant day dream and raised his head to let the Great sergeant know he was listening. "These men have kindly..." Task stopped abruptly as the sound of heavy hooves alerted them to an approaching rider.

The horseman stopped between his countrymen and the strangers. He started speaking quickly to the two tribesmen and Kingswood noticed at once that things were not as friendly. The rider gestured towards the soldiers and whatever was being said, the tribesmen disapproved of it. One even stepped towards the rider and placed his hand on the hilt of the sword until Kingswood heard the word "Murquin".

The tribesmen who were still looking angry, then talked between themselves, one of them said something bitterly to the mounted man and then both turned to Task, spoke briefly and walked away.

"Please excuse, our speaking" said the man with an insincere smile. "My leader asked me to be, as you say- , keeping my eyes open for – an Emissary as yourself". The rider bowed deeply from his saddle at Kingswood as he spoke. "I have been asked to guide you to the camp of Murquin the Overpowerer himself".

The soldiers looked at each other with foreboding glances, then Lieutenant Kingswood spoke first. "Well, thank you, please lead the way, we are very much looking forward to meeting this, Murquin the Overpowerer. Task cast a surprised look at the officer but said nothing.

After a while it was clear they were not heading on the same trail as before. "We are going another way?" asked the Lieutenant as he glanced at Task.

The rider kept trotting forward but turned his head wearing the same insincere smile. "After the attack on your soldiers last time, Murquin the Overpowerer has deemed it – necessary, to avoid, - dangers" the man uttered, although speaking another tongue it was clear to Kingswood that the man was choosing his words carefully.

The two soldiers had now slowed their mounts so their new guide could not hear them.

"We are heading for that small hidden gorge, are we being led into an ambush?" , mumbled Kingswood with his hand covering one side of his mouth.

"I believe so" the Great sergeant replied casually, "The tribesmen suspected something was awry but our guide told them it was not their concern and the wraith of Murquin the Overpowerer would rain down on them and their families if they interfered".

"You heard this and said nothing!!" exclaimed Kingswood in disbelief.

"We have to be certain, if we cast a slight on the honour of these people without cause, we will be in a fight we cannot hope to win. Besides, this man, our guide, does not speak for the tribesmen I am certain, there is something strange about him".

Now Lieutenant Kingswood was quite befuddled, "So we are to walk into trap to find out if this man is untruthful?"

"You learn swiftly" said Task still looking forward, trying not to laugh.

The land was still quite grassy but large boulders were now protruding from the earth and the worn trail they were following led them downwards into the small grassy gorge. Kingswood could see that the gorge twisted steeply this way and that, making it very easy for an attacker to hide around one of the sharp bends.

"Get ready for battle" Task whispered as he craned his head around for signs of danger. "No pretty duels, we watch the back of each other and head for the knoll, they do not want us to reach there for some reason".

"As you say", Kingswood was barely listening, he was already thinking the same but would have given everything he held dear to find the secret of this puzzle.

The sound of snorting mounts, stung the men into action and as three robed riders armed with slender curved swords galloped around a blind bend, Kingswood had his flintlock pistol at the ready.

His shot whistled past the ear of the terrified guide and struck the second rider, the man uttered a shrill cry before he bounced off a large boulder as he fell. "MOVE" roared Task as he dug his heels into the sides of his mount and flew at the other two riders.

The guide had barely unsheathed his own blade as Task elbowed him to his jaw, without halting he held his arm out straight and fired his pistol at the nearest rider and the robed man jumped backwards as if a giant invisible hand had plucked him from his saddle. With the sound of more hooves coming behind him, Kingswood yelled at his own mount and kept with the charging Task, who now unsheathed his plain looking sabre and lashed it across the face of the last rider. They had nearly cleared the gorge when the Lieutenant stopped his mount while handling a small wooden casket from his backpack. As Task screamed at him to keep moving, the officer used his flint lighter to light a short piece of lithe rope hanging from the casket and hurled it onto the trail as the pursuing pack appeared from the last bend. The casket exploded in a black, dirty cloud of smoke and the screams of the horses and men alike signalled the officer's ploy had worked. Whipping his reins against his steed, he rejoined his waiting travelling companion as they headed for the knoll.

"I brought that casket of gunpowder as a gift to the tribal leader we meet" he explained to a puzzled Task, "Thought they could use it for mining or something". Task exhaled loudly, "You took a risk in many ways there Lieutenant".

#

The kindly healer had cleaned his wounds and put some sweet smelling paste on his burnt shoulder. Though now sure he would always have that dark red blotch on his shoulder, he could move it freely with little pain. He was jesting with his comrades when two tribesmen warriors came from the arena entrance and beckoned for the guards to open the cage door of the soldiers.

"You" growled one of the warriors, "Out!, - someone wants, to speak with you".

The men exchanged confused looks as Ben stiffly stepped out of the cage and flanked by the two warriors was led to the arena. The heavy gaol doors were heaved open and as he walked out into the arena, he noticed right away how deserted it was, the silence was quite vexing.

The cavern was not as well lit as what it was when contests took place but Ben who was used to working in the dark, saw Darius sitting on a thick rich looking rug on the arena floor. Sipping some liquid from a fine polished silver goblet he looked up as he saw Ben.

"Sit" he barked as if he was talking to a hound and looked strangely around the arena. "I came by this cavern, a very long time ago" he said thoughtfully as distant memories flooded his head.

"I was a merchant then, never really much of a warrior or skilled with my hands like many of my brethren but I always had grand ideas. "I was also born with, as you say?– a silver tongue" he laughed slightly as he looked Ben in the eye. "A dark hole deep in the bowels of the earth which no one wanted, standing on the crossroads of one of the busiest passages used by the richest of merchants. "I knew those men required rest from a long journey, food, drink, women, - and something to watch to amuse them, and to gamble upon. "So I created this", he said with a glowing smile and gestured around the dark cavern.

"It is hard work" he glowered at Ben as if so he would agree with him. "I organise the best musicians, the best dancers and arrange for the finest food and drink to be brought here".

"As well as the finest cut throats" Ben observed darkly.

"Exactly" nodded Darius enthusiastically clicking his fingers in agreement, "I searched for the most renowed healers, put a reward for the biggest, most voracious beasts to be brought here, I even spend my own time teasing those accursed hyena you have seen".

"You must be so proud" Ben replied in bored voice.

He could see his remark stung his host but the man tried to hide the slight.

"From the gambling, drink, woman and – other – interesting things I find out here, I am the richest man in the desert!, richer than those ancient tribal leader fools!, who only care about honour, their people", Darius made a face like he was going to be sick and drawled on.

"Even richer than most of your, not,- so noble families that bleed the lands dry, leeches, everyone one of them!" , he spat contemptuously on the arena floor.

The man realised he was revealing all that were bottled up inside him, then recovered himself and slowly gave another of his silky grins.

"Everyone leaves me alone here, I have nothing to fear, however..", Ben could see his face had changed slightly and the man looked around the arena uneasily as he lowered his voice. "I helped an old friend with a problem, yet like a stubborn flea on a hound, the problem still, exists. Then there is you!". Darius now stared darkly at Ben like he was the cause of all his recent ill fortunes.

"My talking friend, you come from Eastern Mimas, yet you fight nothing like them. You defeated Tiberius!!, my - own personnel guard, do you know how many men he has bested??, who are you??.

"I am,- a mystery" replied the guardsman, wearing a silly expression, he did not feel like talking to a man like this.

"You entertain my guests well and could be useful to me. Yet", Darius took a deep breath and smiled unpleasantly. "You insult my honour one more time and my guards will take your head and nail it to the gaol door as a warning to others!".

The two guards waiting by his flanks put their hands on the hilt of their swords and another with a bow at the ready, appeared over the edge of the arena from above.

Ben knew he had stepped too far, then realised he was being offered a chance, not a very good chance but a drowning man would take any rope he was given, he thought.

"Please excuse my manners, it has been a difficult few days" he conceded, trying not to show his true feelings, he was now very aware that this man was no fool. "I was captured by slavers in the swampland borders of Callisto and taught skills in combat to increase my value". It is something I do not speak about with others".

"Indeed, I would think you a fool if you did", Darius eyes now sparkled with interest but his voice gave a hint of distrust. "Why spend so much time with the Lion?, I know everything that goes on in the gaol".

Ben smiled faintly and shrugged his shoulders, "It is wise to know ones enemy" he said quietly looking around the now cold, dark arena. "He also gave me some advice on fighting Aaryan the Strong, alas, I did not need it".

This seemed to satisfy Darius. "Yes, I was surprised he defeated Aaryan, but now he is wounded and far from his best. Your wounds do not look severe". Darius glanced over the guardsman slowly.

"I can breathe better through my nose now, the cuts were not deep, I feel ready".

"Good" Darius exclaimed, looking more like his normal assured self. "I would put him in with the hyenas and finish the story now, a lion eaten by hyenas, the thought, it is very jolly, is it not?". He gave a short loud burst of laughter and looked to his guards as he shared the jest with them. However", Darius became serious once more as he spoke slowly, choosing his words carefully. "It would be better if a man killed him, so this Lion would lose his aura of hope before he faded, from memory".

Ben thought this remark was strange but Darius rambled on. "The warriors can bring to the arena, weapons they are used to fighting with, but no muskets, off course. I saw you throw that sword, - Tiberius aside, that would have stuck any man like a bloated pig".

"I can throw knives, I also like to use the same bow and arrows your warriors use" he said hopefully.

"The bow may present, -a risk but throwing knives can be here by sunset and I will arrange time for you to practice with them, well before the contests resume tonight", Darius voice was now eager and excited. "I want this man dead, with or without honour and grace, I care not, do this and you will receive seven easy contests and can leave here a wealthy man and clutching the sword of champions, what do you say?, do we have a deal?".

The eyes of Darius bored into Ben as he spoke, fearing for his life, he tried to mask his true feelings as he spoke again.

"The soldiers I came with...".

"Will never see sunlight again, do we have a deal guardsman?".

"Like any man I value my life more than anything, yes, you have a deal".

#

"This is because I am short, you cannot fool me". Ben stared at Usk in disbelief. Well off course it is because you are short, if you were big this would not work". "You should do what Darius says, then at least one of us will make it out of here alive" said Karl crossly.

125

"None of us will escape if we do that!, we witnessed the ambush, the other tribes would be enraged to hear of such a fiendish act" snarled Usk.

"Or we can do as I suggest and we all have a hope" Ben whispered in their cage.

"A hope?, you have to defeat a great warrior in front of a baying crowd, enter the gaol. Then we have to overpower the guards, get through a locked door that will lead to certain doom, not forgetting escape from a mob of giant warriors which are a match for an army of a hundred!".

Ben realised Usk was speaking sense but tried to ignore the over whelming odds.

"A great man once told me that you can play a devious man's game but do not always need to play by his rules".

"We are doomed!!" stated Karl with his head in his hands.

CHAPTER EIGHT

THE LION AND THE GUARDSMAN

#

Dusk was creeping across Io as Kingswood arched his back and thrust his arms up in a relaxed stretch in front of the big camp fire. He could not believe his luck, fearing the pair would be slain the moment they neared the camp at the top of the knoll, he could not have been more wrong.

One he heard Task shout "EMISSARY" to the advancing warrior tribesmen and some other words in their tongue, they stopped in their tracks and looked at each other.

One of them ran off to fetch someone in charge while the other two gave a short bow to the visitors and respectfully beckoned them forward. The two soldiers were already leading their mounts on foot so to appear less threatening, a moment later several young men came along and gently took the reins and took the mounts away to be fed and watered. The explosion had startled the men at the camp but later Task had explained that once the tribesmen were confident that the intentions of the visitors were sincere, they sent out their warriors to discover who would dare to attack men under a banner of peace.

"They told me there were no bodies to be found" said Task as he munched on some dates. "Only several dead mounts and plenty of blood, your gunpowder certainly did the trick!" he added with an admiring tone.

Kingswood was now feeling at ease with the Great sergeant, he was an experienced soldier who knew well the tongue and customs of these people. He was also an impressive warrior himself but like the great warriors, once away from danger, the man was calm and still watchful.

"Strange that they took the bodies when they fled" he asked thinking hard.

"I said there was something strange about the guide" reminded Task gently glancing around the camp. "He was not honourable or dignified like the tribesmen I have met before, more of a jackal instead of a wolf".

"Meaning, the men he was with...".

"Are not from around here, I can promise you that Lieutenant".

"Where are they from then" asked Kingswood sitting up right to concentrate better.

"I fear we will find out soon and by heaven we best be prepared when we do".

#

The men in the gaol were now fearful and uneasy, the noise of sickening laughter and cheering that drifted into the cave, informed them that the contests were once more due to commence.

As promised Darius had five shiny bladed, light brown wooden handled, sleek knives lying in their own freshly made leather shoulder strap waiting for Ben in the middle of the arena. He was summoned there once more by the two guards but this time there was no gloating face to welcome him. There was even a figure made of straw but clad in robes, hanging from the wooden ladder for practice. The knives were slightly heavier than he was used to using but well crafted. After sliding on the thick shoulder strap and adjusting it so it was comfortable, all five blades were soon in the middle of the chest of the straw warrior. "However, figures made of straw do not fight back" he jested to himself but was well satisfied with his new weapons.

Afterwards, Ben was granted a specially requested lavish meal of meat and herbs, which he shared with his comrades when the guards were not looking.

"Eat" he commanded Karl quietly, "you will need all your strength when we escape. Can you even move?", he questioned as he glanced over the wounded soldier, whose cuts were healing but still moaned in discomfort when he sat upright.

"I can bloody well move out of here" he grinned through gritted teeth.

"He will do what needs to be done" Usk assured the guardsman in a forceful tone as he gave his friend a pointed nod.

Eventually a guard signalled to Ben that he would be fighting soon. He stood up and started to stretch his muscles. With his left wrist he steered his right arm across his chest, his muscles felt good but his left shoulder still felt raw and very sore.

"The guard strode purposefully over as usual and unlocked the cage door and pulled it open, without an invitation the guardsman stepped briskly from his prison for the last time. He was joined by the Lion who would not look at him but merely kept his eyes on the doors, his body seemed relaxed but his face was a mask of fierce concentration. There were no displays of aggression or uncontrolled anger, both fighters were saving their strength and kept their minds clear for the trial ahead.

They were hit by a wall of noise that made Ben shudder, such was the ferocity of it. The throng of exuberant spectators made the previous ones seem meek and timid by comparison.

"I bet you think you will have increased your wealth greatly after tonight" Ben shouted at the host but nothing could be heard. "If I am to perish here, you will come through the gates of hell with me!" he promised to the figure who looked like he had never been happier or more excited. Ben wore the shoulder belt under his tunic with the knives, a guard had sneaked them in as the Lion was surrounded by the other guards who taunted him under the instruction of Darius.

Out of respect for this person who he liked after their brief meeting, he was determined only to use the knives if the contest turned against him, which he suspected tonight, it may. He fought to clear the words that he used in the gaol that flooded through his head as he tried to prepare for this dangerous opponent.

They may want you to play their game but you need not play by their rules.

It entered his mind like a blow to his head and he now knew the only way they could escape.

"He wants both of us dead, If we unite, we can escape through the gaol" He pleaded loudly to the lion.

"Do not waste your lies on me, I thought you had honour until you met Darius", the man replied bitterly shaking his head.

Darius announced the warriors and drowned the voices of both men.

"MY FRIENDS WE BEGIN THE NIGHT WITH THE CONTEST OF THE YEAR". Darius was in full swagger and was clearly enjoying himself.

"WE HAVE THE ALL CONQUERING LION OF THE UNDERWORLD HIMSELF, SEVEN TIMES VICTOR HERE, - PITTED AGANIST THE SLAYER OF TIBERIUS THE TORMENTOR, I PRESENT ONCE MORE, THE GUARDSMAN OF MIMAS!!".

"Eastern Mimas" Ben mumbled to himself as he kept his gaze on the Lion who now stood in a very narrow stance but his eyes were like burning orbs, such were the concentration.

"ONLY ONE MAN WILL LEAVE THE ARENA ALIVE ".

He stopped to control his excitement and then gave the awaited command to the fighters.

The two men threw themselves at their weapons. Ben dived at his, snatched them up and rolled forwards to his feet. In an attempt to knock the blade from the grasp of his foe he surged forward, only to have his own straight bladed sword whipped out of his hand. He side stepped, white with fear as his adversary hurtled past him, a streak of crimson appeared across his torso as if by a magical hand.

With a vice like two handed grip on his long slender curved blade, the man was powerful for his size and very swift. The warriors now slowly, wearily, circled each other slowly.

The wound was not deep and Ben glanced for his guardsman sword only to see that it had broken in two. The blade must have struck a rock, the swords were often dismissed for their poor quality in Eastern Mimas. So he kept circling, his steps were light, his feet poised for sudden movement. Though battered and bruised, this man seemed unhindered in momement. To his dismay he noticed the Lion's movements were mirroring his own, he matched Ben step for step as if part of a macabre game. The guardsman was entranced how the Lion kept his sword in the same two handed grip but held it low and away from his opponent.

To his annoyance he found himself playing the game of this creative warrior and charged at the man with a bellowing battle cry in order to break the spell.

The lion did not move, his eyes showed no emotion, Ben thought the man had frozen and continued his attack. He raised his sword to strike only for his new foe to parry his blow to the ground, spin around and sliced the guardsmans lower back with a rapier counter attack. Ben nearly dropped his sword as his whole body went rigid as a bolt of searing agony shot through his back. Out of instinct he forced himself to stumbled forwards as the blade of the Lion scythed through the air once more, missing the back of his opponents neck by a hairs breath. He doggedly turned around to face this most deadly of adversaries and felt the thick leather knife strap loosen from his torso. His back was bleeding but not severed in two as the strike had been meant to achieve.

Relief and renewed hope flooded his body as he realised how lucky he had been.

His heart pounding relentlessly he glanced over his attacker with great satisfaction to see that the man was befuddled to why he was still standing.

"A MAN OF YOUR WISDOM AND YOU STILL NOT UNDERSTAND??" the guardsman roared with real fire in his eyes. "THE DRAUGHT IN YOUR WATER, WHY THEY NEVER LET YOU REST??, AARYAN THE STRONG!!, HE WILL NEVER LET YOU LEAVE HERE!!". THEY EVEN TRIED TO CAPTURE THE WHITE PRINCESS!!. Ben backed slowly away to show that this was no trick.

Darius could not hear what was being said but he could read men better than any parchment. He hastily beckoned over one of his warriors, "Get the bowmen ready" he ordered, his steely gaze still on the contestants.

"Master, I do not understand..."

"The bowman now or the Hyenas will be stripping the flesh of your bones next!", Darius rasped, glowering at the poor warrior.

The Lion swiftly recovered his wits, "you see me as a fool?", he did not shout but his words still carried to his enemy.

"I know Darius wants me to die here but I must be victorious, then, they will have to listen to me!!".

Ben did not understand but he had already made up his mind on what had to be done. He switched his sword to his left hand and swivelled on his rear heel and dashed towards the guards by the gaol doors. The nearest one had his hand on the hilt of his sheathed sword as a brown handled knife flew into his throat. The stricken man was already falling to his knees as Ben clumsily span around and threw a second then a third shiny blade into the rear leg, then the chest of the remaining guard.

The blood was now seeping freely from both his wounds and Ben struggled with the giant heavy wooden bolt, he heard light footsteps behind him but knew he could not defend himself in time. Suddenly the corner of the arena went dark as the flaming torch to the right of Ben was extinguished, then the Lion was standing right next to him, helping to heave the bolt to one side.

"Get inside swiftly, Darius will have alerted the ", a loud thud interrupted the Lion as a heavy arrow barely missed Ben's head and was now embedded in the door.

The Lion pulled the iron ring with a grunt and both men scrambled inside as a flurry of familiar thuds peppered the thick doors.

Once inside the grunting man struggled to pull the same door close, as the guardsman who was now feeling weaker by the moment gazed at the gaol dumbfounded.

The first cage his eyes fell on was filled by the two burly guards, Usk was leaning on the cage with a triumphant grin, twilling a ring of keys around on a finger.

"You were right, I could fit past that bent bar that Aaryan mangled, it turned out that even his friends wanted to escape this pit as well" he beamed.

Ben groggily looked around to see that all the prisoners were now at the far end of the cave, armed and looked very keen to escape.

"Less talk and more haste!", smiled the Lion as he grabbed several bales of straw kept to one side of the cave for bedding and heaved them against the doors. He plucked one of the lanterns from the wall and threw it with all his might. It shattered, as it struck the doors and the burning oil spilled across the doorway lighting the hay and the wooden doors as it flowed.

"GO" shouted the Lion to the others, "THERE IS NO TURNING BACK NOW!!, THEY WILL NOW SLAUGHTER ANY PRISONER THEY FIND!". His serious face faded and his voice became gentle and friendly.

"Could you lead your friends to the back with the others" he asked politely of Usk.

"There are some items, we will -need here, before we start our journey".

Usk nodded respectfully and heaved himself under Karl's shoulder and the three soldiers made their way to the now battered down door at the rear of the cave.

When they passed through it, Ben was dismayed to see the other men were still standing there. Usk cursed loudly and pushed his way past two men to reveal a collection of metal cages and heavy wooden fences in this much wider cave.

Ben nearly dropped down dead to the see the three monstrous Hyenas locked in the same study looking iron barred cage, snarling and snapping at the terrified new guests. As well as the hyenas, the men were also now staring at some fenced in wild boar, with tusks like curved daggers and the biggest, most evil looking black bull Ben had ever laid eyes on. The beast had thick white horns the height of a mans torso and vast muscles bulged beneath the bulls black coat.

"What is the delay!" snapped Usk in disbelief at the nearest man rooted to his spot.

"We can hear footsteps of warriors coming up the passage, we are trapped" protested the man fearfully.

There was a deathly silence as the sound of heavy footsteps became deafening as Ben spoke, "How did you hunt bear in deep undergrowth in Diore?" he asked softly.

Usk was stunned by this question. "With - hounds off course", he answered slowly, thinking this was not the time to discuss pastimes.

"Oh, I think we can do better than hounds" Ben smiled wickedly.

#

Bold and powerful, the tribal warriors were relishing the forth coming battle.

"Around the bend and we will deliver them an honourable death,- which is their right as true warriors" observed the leader, Ahmad, respectfully. The strongest and most skilful man among them, he was respected and feared equally by the warriors. He turned to his trusted companion by his side.

"You look worried my friend, we have fought many battles together, there is nothing worse to fear here".

"It is these cursed passages, I like my fighting under the sun or the stars, not in these cramp stone tombs" muttered the man as he peered anxiously in the gloom holding a flaming torch in one hand and his trusted blade in the other.

The big leader smiled at this. "A battle is a battle, we cannot always choose the place, it will.." he stopped abruptly, "They are coming, ready yourselves!" he whispered back to his men. "Wait, that sounds more like..., MOVE!!, - TO THE WALLS!, NOW!" he bellowed, as the sound of heavy crashing hooves echoed down the passage. He rushed to the side pinning his comrade to wall as the bull slid around the corner. Snorting heavily like a mythical dragon, dark as night, eyes wide with terror, it exploded into a terrifying charge, lowering it's massive head close to the ground.

His sharp reactions saved him and his loyal friend but alas, the following warriors were not so fortunate. The heavy thud of one man being hit head on and the bones breaking of another as he was flung against a wall was swiftly followed by the agonising cries of a third man as he was gored on the ground. Ahmad cursed loudly but as he stepped from the wall he then had to throw himself to the other side of the passage as high pitched calls announced the arrival of the Boar.

Knocking one tusk away with his sword, the leader swivelled around on his hips and kicked the Boar hard on his ribs.

Squealing horribly the pig did not stop and the herd flowed on, toppling the remaining warriors who were still standing like spinning wooden tops.

Looking over at his groaning friend who had been knocked down by a particularly heavy boar, Ahmad gave a forced dry smile.

He had barely uttered the fateful words, "Well, it could have been worse" in a reluctant tone when an inhuman chattering chilled his body to the bone. He rose to his feet as the scrambling of blunt powerful claws on stone urged him to ready his sword. The blade only got as far as his thigh, as a heavy muzzle clamped his arm like an iron trap and the weapon fell clattering to the ground as his forearm broke into two.

At the far end of the passage way, the cries of the men being trampled underfoot by the rampaging beasts alerted the guards outside. Letting their brethren run pass them, their act of compassion failed to reward them kindly.

"CLOSE THE DOOR, YOU FOOLS" wailed one bruised and bloodied man as he stumbled past them. The guards snapped into action pushing the heavy wooden door shut only to be knocked down as the door was torn from the hinges, crushing them underneath. Still the black raging beast did not slow down and charged onwards to freedom.

Still in the passageway, the progress of the soldiers was not as swift. The others had been running behind the animals with their torches waving wildly and shouting so hard their throats became painful. Ben still felt unsteady on his feet and the badly wounded Karl was still limping with Usk under his right shoulder to support him.

"Hurry, we are not safe here" urged the Lion who had caught up with them.

"Even I could have told you that -, LOOK OUT!!", Karl wrenched himself from his friend and lashed out at the battered warrior now standing before them. The attacker parried the tired sword thrust and arced his long slender blade across the belly of Karl. Usk threw himself at the assailant with the fury of a demon and tackled him to the ground as the Lion shouted a warning to their rear. He sprang sideways and with his twin handed grip smashed the hilt of his sword into the attackers face.

Desperate to avenge his friends death, he rushed forwards regardless, only to feel Ben's blade slash across his chest.

"I am sorry!!" he said firmly as the Lion gave him a look of disgust. "Look!, you lot are too good to play with, we need to escape now!!".

"Only the three of us now" spat Usk, his fallen comrade in his arms.

Ben took a deep breath, "Here, let me help".

"I have him!", the sergeant from Diore snapped as he turned sharply away from Ben's outstretched hands.

The escapees silently passed the remaining wounded and dazed warriors to emerge through to the outside world. Trampling over the guards still groaning under the heavy door, they looked for signs of danger but could only hear the sound of metal on metal and war cries from the brightly lit campsite below them.

"They are after the horses but few will leave that camp now" the Lion stated in a voice full of remorse.

"Well, that is where we are heading, is it not?, we need mounts to get away from here as swiftly as we can before sunset!", asked Ben wearing a befuddled face.

"Steal mounts yes, but over there, where Darius has his own personnel camp, for discussing – matters of wealth". The Lion pointed to a camp fire, to the right of the main campsite.

"Good, I wanted to meet that fat weasel on my own terms, Time to right some wrongs" Ben's tone was determined and hard edged. He glanced down at one of the fallen warriors and shakily, ripped free the mans bow and quiver.

"He has more blood on his hands that you will ever know but after what you said about the White Princess, we must escape swiftly tonight, to prevent the fall of at least two kingdoms!"

"Escape swiftly?, I will bury Karl first, then if they find me I will die with a sword in my hand, like a true soldier of Diore". Usk was wiping a tear from his eye but looked resolute.

"We cannot wait and we will not leave you, he would want you escape" protested Ben urgently.

"Your friend died bravely in battle, the others will respect that greatly, he will have – an honourable burial" the Lion added, still peering into the darkness for advancing warriors.

"Can I at least say farewell, we became soldiers at the same time" Usk said weakly, his strong stance was ebbing away as he gazed down on his fallen friend.

"We will meet you down there, on the right of his camp", Ben passed them both and put a firm hand on the sergeants shoulder. "He did Diore proud".

Now allies, the Lion and the guardsman walked silently down the slope towards the camp of Darius. It was not easy in the gloom but they took extra care with each step, they were perhaps too cautious Ben thought, the clash of blades could still be heard but the sound was dwindling. The war cries also now seemed like screams and his heart sunk for the fate of the other escaped prisoners.

#

The warrior had made sure both mounts had been well watered but he still felt uneasy.

"Everything is how you ordered it Master" he stooped with a low bow. "But I beg you to reconsider, with the prisoners roaming free, it would be wise to wait until first light".

"Wait?" snapped Darius reproachfully. "When Mugrin the Overpowerer hears what has happened this night, I will be nothing but a spirit wandering these lands!!. Now go back and bring my strong box. The sleeping draught you poured in the well should be taking affect now, when they wake up tomorrow, we will be very far from here and they will have no idea in which direction. As the man left briskly, Darius stared into the darkness.

"You have brought destruction on my world guardsman" he hissed bitterly, then gave a resentful chuckle.

"You think you have won??, I will use every piece of my wealth, contact every merchant I know. I will –have your beating heart ripped from your chest when you least expect it, your family, your friends, will suffer a wrath so great-, Oh, what was that?".

The first hyena sank his teeth in the right leg of Darius and his shrill scream pierced far into the night sky. As his body hit the ground, the second hyena latched onto one of his flailing arms and chewed on it, crunching the limb like a twig. His shrieks continued, as pinned down, he could barely look up to see the bulging, slavering jaws of the third beast closing around his throat.

"That was Darius" exclaimed the Lion, staring to where the cries came from. "The Hyenas must have him."

"Who knows who the ghastly hand of death touches next!" replied Ben coldly as he nocked an arrow ready into his new bow

The Lion smiled but as he spoke there was urgency in his voice.

"This way quickly" he commanded, "Darius would only be outside the camp on a night like this for one reason, he is trying to escape, unseen, we may have found our horses!". Running as hard as they could without falling over, they found the waiting mounts tied to a bush. They could not see Darius or the hyenas but could hear the sickening crunching of bones being broken up nearby. Footsteps made Ben spin around and he instinctively let fly. The guard dropped a small wooden treasure box and fell backwards in the earth.

"The spirits are with us tonight. My name is Mansour, you have many skills my friend".

"Finding despair is one of them", he stopped suddenly and twisted his body towards more footsteps. He barely managed to hold onto the arrow as he just made out the figure of Usk.

"You nearly killed me" he exclaimed, in a hurt but also angry tone.

"To be fair I aim at their chest, so this one would have gone way over your head!" mocked the guardsman, happy to see the likeable fellow once more.

All three laughed as Mansour grabbed the reins of the mounts.

"We should leave right now, before the hyenas finish their meal" he laughed once more as he clambered painfully on a mount as Ben got on the second with the same discomfort. Now that fighting seemed unlikely he was feeling tired and his wounds seem to hurt more than ever.

Usk sprang on the back of his mount as they trotted off into the depths of the night.

#

"Sending those mercenaries across the border with that paid killer was a childish mistake on your part – but what you are saying now- I cannot believe the Archduke has given his blessing to such, a murderous – plot".

Lieutenant Otto's face was pale as he paced back and forth in the huge brown tent, shaking his head in disbelief.

Leon however, looked quite calm as he fiddled with a strange looking polished barrelled pistol. His eyes flickered with joy as he adjusted a screw in the handle of the small but peculiar weapon.

"His Imperial and Royal Highness thinks the same as I, we now have no need of the tribesmen as allies. They could have a vast empire as they did in times long ago. Instead they sit around their camp fires carving their little wooden pipes.." Leon babbled on as the Lieutenant grew impatient.

"With their warriors and their wise men on our side, we would be unstoppable but if your idea goes ahead, there will be nothing but wars and endless bloodshed in the desert. No passage of trade would be possible!!." The officer renown for his calm in the heat of battle was beginning to lose his. This little weasel did not even bother looking up as he spoke to him, just played with his little toy as if it was the only thing that mattered.

"This is my latest invention" he said proudly wiping the long shiny barrel with a special piece of cloth.

"I am especially pleased with it, it does not look much but the enemy officer would think the same.., until one pulls the trigger and this beauty hits the dumb soldier full in the chest at much greater distances than other pistols. Not only that", his glinting hazel eyes admired his own work with intense satisfaction. "When the projectile hits the target, the metal is so soft it spreads instead of passing through, massive loss of blood I guarantee!".

Lieutenant Otto was dumb founded, "are you sick?" he enquired, whilst trying to conceal his loathing of this nasty creature.

Still inspecting the pistol, Leon rambled on as if he had not heard the last few words.

"We will no longer require the trade passage through those desert wastelands, our sea trade will soon continue to flow as in our glorious days of old".

"But the Sea Raiders.."

"Defeated in two recent sea battles and our port in Marlborough sank their flagship by itself!".

Otto was blown away with shock, "But how?, why did we not get to hear such wonderful news" he asked in a mixture of surprise and anger.

"I myself, have developed a projectile like the baby one we have here, that can sink enemy ships before they can get close enough to fire themselves" he boasted as he finally looked up to acknowledge the presence of the officer.

"However, the projectile is not soft and the explosive inside is an extremely powerful one, - that again, I have made. As for the secrecy, Mimas will only know of our newly restored power when our armies are massing on their own pitiful borders".

The officer could no longer hold back his emotions as he stared at the man in front of him with firery contempt.

"Inventing these weapons of destruction is not enough for you is it Leon?, you must see the death and suffering that they cause. That is why you invented this plot and persuaded his Highness, the Archduke to put you in charge of it". Otto spoke with confidence as he finally worked out in his mind what had been happening.

"Not bad for a dumb soldier" sneered Leon, "However, if this destruction and suffering is too, - cold blooded for you. I can always ask for someone who will follow orders and merely arrange my protection".

Rage bubbled up throughout his controlled calm body and the Lieutenant leaned over the source of his tension. He just managed to control himself and remember his upbringing and officer training and gave a forced smile.

"Oh, I follow orders and I will keep you safe, I am a true professional. You will be wise to remember that when folk who you have never met before are trying to murder you where you stand, inventor!". The officer made no attempt to walk around the shocked man as he shoulder barged past his fellow country man with little effort. Not used to anyone speaking back to him, Leon stopped smirking and watched the experienced officer stride out of his tent, marking his sensible words.

CHAPTER NINE

MUQRIN THE OVERPOWERER

Ben woke up feeling very hot and his bare chest was drenched in sweat, his head was beating like a drum.

"You have a fever", came a soft voice behind him. He sensed he was in no danger but felt too weak to do anything even if he wanted.

"Your wounds are now healing well, you –cared after your chest wound, but it was the small-, as you say, cut?, on your lower back that caused the infection.

He groaned in disgust, he had been told countless times that even small cuts can be harmful on a long journey if not cared for.

He was so weary he had forgotten a very important lesson.

"Thank you", the guardsman at least still had the common sense not to get up this time. He looked around to see where he was to. He was lying under the shade of a large earth coloured tent but not like one he had ever seen before. This one seemed to have a high peak above him where he lay but as he craned his head carefully to either side, he could see the sides sloped crookedly down to the ground. There was a strange smell which reminded him of live stock for some reason but as he rested on a thick soft carpet, his head propped up by huge padded cushions and covered to his stomach by soft silk sheets, he had never been so comfortable.

"The soft voice continued.

"Please lay still, you will, get better, I have made this potion that will make you recover, more swiftly. "Forgive -my words" the man mumbled apologetically.

Ben smiled kindly, these folk tried so hard to speak his tongue well and he knew none of their words, yet - they were the ones who were sorry!!.

As the elderly sloping figure departed, another man came in. Dressed in a pristine long white tunic peering out from a white sleeveless cloak and a short headdress circled by a black and brown headband. Clean shaven, his square jaw jutted out proudly but his emerald eyes still flashed brightly as before.

"Mansour?" croaked Ben in surprise and awe, he tried to sit up swiftly but just as swiftly regretted it.

"Lay still, were the words of the healer I believe, and you people say we cannot understand your tongue" he exclaimed loudly rolling his eyes at the same time.

The guardsman gave a restrained chuckle, "I take it, I have you to thank for the healer, how long have I been here?.

"Two days, Marc stopped you falling from your saddle, sharp wits that man".

Who is Marc?" asked Ben groggily.

"Sergeant Usk!, you soldiers should talk to each other more you know, it is the only way you learn" he gave a hearty laugh. "Here I will help you drink the potion now, we must leave at daybreak".

Ben could sense the man was vexed but the potion went down sweetly and he drifted back to sleep.

#

Eventually he woke again and felt quite refreshed but still weak, the fever had gone but his wound was still throbbing fiercely, his head clear, he could see it was dark outside. Again Mansour came in at the right time and flashed a comforting smile.

"You may have saved my life and I owe that healer a debt as well" he said reaching out for a flask of water next to his bed.

"You helped me escape the Underworld, you owe me nothing. The healer however, I gave him a gem from Darius's strong box, that paid for his services and his silence. I also required some – help".

Ben had forgotten that Mansour was hurt from the contest with Aaryan the Strong but showed little of it in their own contest. Gazing at this inspiration of a man, he could see the bruises were merely a light yellow colour on the side of his face now.

Then a thought had hit him like a quarter staff. "You said two days!!, I need to return to the river, post haste, to stop a war!".

"We, - must stop a war", Mansour corrected firmly. "These senseless acts by Muqrin to gain power will pour devastation among our lands".

"Muqrin" enquired Ben weakly, his mind was now racing once more.

"Muqrin the Overpowerer is the leader of the five hills tribe. He has long desired to be the first Emir for over ten score years to rule these lands, he must be stopped at any cost!!". His bravery is accepted without question by the tribal leaders because he was the first man to leave the Underworld with ten victories".

Ben could see Mansour was deep in thought.

"Is that why you were in the Underworld?, so you could gain the respect to lead" he asked hopefully. "Since we have met, I have harboured much respect for your words and your actions, not just your fighting skill". He stopped abruptly. He was not good with words and feared he had said too much.

Mansour beamed broadly, "Your words warm me, my friend but I am no leader. I spoke out against Muqrin and rode to meet the leaders of the other tribes to talk peace".

"What happened?".

"On my journey to meet them I was attacked by Aaryan, his brother and the two others you saw at the gaol. I escaped by slaying his brother but was then ambushed by some of Dariurs's men who had been following. While I waited in my cage in the gaol, Aaryan was brought in, he said they attacked me for a reward but now he would spill my blood for nothing".

The guardsman was now befuddled. "So Darius wanted you to - vanish, - to please this Muqrin?, so who commanded Aaryan to kill you?"."Alas, that I do not know" mumbled Mansour.

"Well, at least I am not the only one everyone is trying to kill", Ben said out loud in a dry voice.

#

Titan, though still lame, was now pulling hard. A thick rope hung from the heavy harness he was wearing, the other end was tightly wrapped around the massive forearms of Muqrin. His feet sliding through the stony ground as he resisted the mighty beast as much as any man could.

"This animal is magnificent" he panted heavily, he had little breath and his huge dome head and bare torso was dripping with sweat. Every muscle was bulging, as he leaned back to slow his pace.

"You must rest my Master, you push yourself too hard.

Several men immediately grabbed the reins of Titan and another two helped to take the ropes of Muqrin.

"You know why I must push myself so hard" he accepted a towel from one of the men and wiped his head and neck.

"You are the greatest warrior in all of Io, my Master, soon you will be Emir, you will need all your time to rule", Farouk said these words quietly but wanted the words to be marked by his beloved Master.

"I am not Emir yet" barked the heavy man but then regretted his tone.

"You see the desert Lion as I do Farouk, when he is young and strong nothing stands in his way, then he gets older and slower.., then he lives in fear. Always in fear of the younger males strutting into his realm, he defeats the first one, then the second but one day he will lose. Does he have an honourable death, no, he stumbles from his kingdom, a matter of amusement for the other beasts, even the jackal will steal from him now".

Farouk had heard this before but still the pain hurt more than a hot blade skewering his hand.

"My Master, please do not speak like this, you can nearly touch that many only have dreamt about". He then glanced around to confirm that the men had left them to look after Titan and the other horses.

"There, is a messenger who brings grave tidings of Darius" he whispered and beckoned over a tribesman who waited respectfully twenty paces away.

He ran over and bowed deeply. The man kept his eyes at the ground as he spoke, his voice wavered.

"I regret to say that Darius cannot be found, some men escaped from the caves, there was a battle, almost all of them died but- we think wild beasts may have him, judging by the trail we found".

Muqrin knew that every tribesman never referred to The Underworld by name but merely as the caves. His eyes narrowed on the messenger, his rage was building.

"Almost, all of them?" he echoed, his voice rumbled like thunder.

"Two horses were missing, as well as the strong box Darius always kept close to him. We lost many men, we could not search properly...".

"Enough", Muqrin took such a deep breath it looked as if he would swallow the shaking messenger whole.

He snapped his fingers and one of his men ran over.

"See this man has some water and feed him well, he has been riding hard, now leave us!".

Surprised by the gesture, Farouk began stumbling his words.

"My Master, let me take some warriors, we will search thoroughly, if he has escaped, he cannot be far".

"FAR???", roared his Master, his veins bulging around his trunk- like neck.

"He will head towards my camp on the knoll, he will have learnt that the tribal leaders are due to meet there in two days time. I will face him there and finish this myself!, without the scheming Darius and WITHOUT ANY FURHER ATTACKS ON HIM!!".

The tall gangly man stepped back in shock.

"You knew my Master?, I meant no dishonour, you were trying to get the other leaders on your side, you could not be distracted, Aaryan the Strong was the ideal choice to crush Mansour-"

"SILENCE!!, you know never to use his name in front of me. His name means victory, HE – WILL NEVER –GAIN –VICTORY-IN THESE LANDS". His giant frame trembled, his face flushed with fury.

"You have angered me, Farouk!, any other man I would have carved him in two. Now leave me".

Farouk felt as if his heart had been ripped from his chest and he bowed deeply and walked away from his Master.

Murqrin the Overpowerer looked into the distance, "I must learn to rein in this temper of mine" he snarled. "First I will cut down my enemy, then,- I will learn to rein in this temper of mine".

#

Ben and Mansour sat on thick decorative rugs as they eat their breakfast on the hard rocky ground. It was still dark but the first glow of the sun crept slowly over the desert. Usk had already eaten and was being shown a strange beast by a friend of Mansour, Aamir.

A dark brown colour, the beast seem to be lying on it's knees but with an unnaturally long neck and a massive shaggy mound on the back, it loomed over the amazed sergeant. Aamir who was typical of his brethren, not as tall but perhaps bigger limbed, seemed very amicable and slapped his hand on parts of the creature as he spoke in his own tongue slowly.

"Aamir is a very trusted friend who I have known a long time" said Mansour as he sipped his tea. "He wanders the desert and sees and hears everything. It was he who told me about the meeting of the leaders. He has sent messages to the other leaders with his falcon. He will come with us but we should leave soon. How do you feel?".

"I feel as if I have been to hell and Back!" he smiled grimly, "but I must go. When my Lieutenant hears what

Sergeant Usk and I have to say, he will move heaven and earth to stop the fighting.

"He sounds like a good man" observed Mansour, "alas, it may not be so easy from my side.

"This Muqrin the Overpowerer does not seem like a man who does what he is asked".

"You are not wrong my friend. As his accuser, he will have the right to challenge me in combat".

"He has won ten victories in the Underworld!. I do not think he would use the name The Overpowerer for merriment".

"Again you are right" sighed Mansour heavily, "yet I have no choice". His mood then changed slightly, "Ah but what was I thinking, I had forgotten something".

He stood up and walked over to his mount and took a long black sack hanging from the saddle. To Ben's surprise he pulled out the gleaming Champion of the Underworld sword. It looked even more sublime in the emerging daylight and the etchings on the blade seem to pull his attention towards them.

"This is yours, Darius was a greedy fool but he paid the finest sword smith to create this".

Smiling, Mansour presented the weapon to a bemused Ben who had sprung up from the campfire. His hand gripped the hilt lightly and he turned the blade to marvel the beauty of it. The sword had perfect balance and seemed so light in his palm as he tried to feel the weight. In many ways it was strikingly similar to the curved sword he was given, except this one had a polished metal handle instead of a dour wooden one and was shiny and new, not worn looking. Stepping away from Mansour he practised a couple of half hearted cuts with the Champion of the Underworld sword and was mesmerized.

He hesitated and shook his head.

"If this sword is truly for the Champion of the Underworld, then it should be yours. You had more victories than I, you had bested me.."

"If you were not trying to escape, your sword blows may have been more precise, besides I am not a warrior, nor do I wish to be remembered as such".

Ben nearly burst out laughing but realised just in time this man was not jesting.

"You are a great warrior, your moves are like the wind".

Mansour had become serious and glowered into the fading fire.

"It is difficult to explain", at that moment Aamir called over to his friend and Mansour nodded slightly and jumped to his feet.

"Come, we must get ready to leave here, we sit around talking like old men while the fate of our lands hang in the balance!".

As they set off, Ben glanced around at the surrounding landscape. He could see no trees or grass of any kind, just vast expanses of sand and stony ground. It looked forbidding and harsh but it was also tranquil and he liked the peace.

The men rode in single file so there was not much chance for talking. Mansour was leading while Aamir stayed at the back with his incredible beast. Usk was on another horse that Aamir always kept just in case. Such was the distance the travellers slowly trotted on until Aamir shouted a warning as he saw something far behind them. Ben turned his head to see an enormous wall of brown cloud advancing silently behind them.

"DRAGONSTORM" cried Mansour as he whirled around in his saddle, then pointed to a large rocky outcrop on a small hill, a little way to their right.

"THERE, NOW!!, AS IF YOUR LIVES DEPENDED ON IT!".

Without question the party galloped towards the peak, to Ben's surprise, Aamir overtook them and as he reached the rocks he led his beast behind a huge boulder and waved the others in.

As they dismounted, Aamir shepherded them towards the middle of the rocks and thrust a big blanket and a cask of water to each of them in turn. The sand was now whipping around their ears and hardly anything could be heard over the howling wind.

"MAY LAST FOR DAYS, SAND WILL BLIND YOU!!, STAY UNDER BLANKET AND DO NOT MOVE!, MOVE AND YOU WILL PERISH!!", bellowed Aamir amidst the din. Ben backed himself against a big oval shaped boulder and pulled the blanket over his whole body as instructed. He thought a hollow in the ground would be the best place for a storm like this but there had been no time to argue. He clenched his teeth as he could feel the sand stabbing the blanket with no idea of what was to come next.

#

He had been holding onto the blanket for grim death what seemed for an eternity, his eyelids seemed as heavy as iron shutters and after some uncontrolled sleepy nods he succumbed to his weariness.

#

"Good Afternoon sergeant Hawks of the Civil Mountain Guard" came a cheerful voice accompanied by a hard shove. Ben woke up with a start and carefully peeled down his blanket to see Mansour standing over him.

"Good afternoon??, how long?" he was still groggy with sleep.

"One day but this is good, in some parts of the desert the Dragon storm may pass on for many days.".

"One day! But we will miss the meeting" blurted the guardsman.

Mansour smiled with confidence..

"There is always a way, there is a whole moon tonight, we will travel under it."

"How will we find our way, the landscape is all the same around here!".

"Have faith my friend, not my first time in the desert!".

They watered their mounts and had started off once more. Surprisingly the faith seemed to grow on everybody, especially Usk who Aamir had allowed to ride his humped beast. Ben could not help but snigger to himself as he kept hearing the words, "who is the tallest now!, you are not so tall" coming from behind him at height.

Eventually nightfall came and the guardsman was awe struck by the magnificent views. The ghostly white moon seemed to sit on a high sandy ridge in front of them like a gigantic orb, the ground was all sandy and flat as Mansour and Ben rode next to each other. The dark sky was filled with thousands of diamond like stars.

"See those stars in a group over there?" exclaimed Mansour brightly, "they tell us we need to travel over that ridge to reach the camp". He then went on in some detail about what some of the stars meant in the lore of his people.

"Amazing" muttered a dumb founded guardsman.

"My father taught me all this when I was but a child" he said with pride. "He was a warrior, a legendary warrior. After each meal he would give me instruction on fighting with the blade but said I did not have to follow his footsteps, a fulfilled man chooses his own path, he always said". "He knew I enjoyed poetry and helping other tribes, creating deeper wells, building machines to lift heavy stone and so forth.

Ben gave a befuddled look and Mansour laughed.

"Poetry is important among the tribes" he explained, "it is a good way to reach out to people, to inform them of matters".

"Yet, you are masterful with a sword?".

Mansour shrugged his shoulders, "I watch what people and even the animals do in life, how they move, how they behave. In the desert it can help people, in a contest, I can see a move by my opponent before he does it".

"That would help greatly" Ben observed lightly. Sitting in the saddle listening to this man he felt a fool after believing some of the dumb stories he had heard before. This was a man who embraced knowledge and wisdom but still spoke proudly of his ancestors beliefs.

"There are some people still in the dark ages and it is not them!" he muttered to himself.

"Did you say something" enquired Mansour politely, "sometimes I do misunderstand your tongue".

"I trust you have not flayed anyone here for a long time" he asked by means of jesting about himself.

"Flayed, we would not flay anyone, that is barbaric!. Stories from different lands can be based on untruths. I heard tales about the Civil Mountain Guard, but we do not discuss them, it would be insulting. One of them is that they think of you all as mad."

"People can be ill-informed".

"Inbred rabble was another".

"Envy can be an unpleasant thing".

"Even say that your soldiers talk to their mounts all day as if they think they will talk back.".

Ben went to open his mouth but said nothing, went to speak again, then made a strange expression as he looked back to the stars and stayed silent.

The two men then glanced at each other and laughed hard.

The air was cool, the silver landscape so beautiful, gazing up at the brightly lit heavens made Ben wished he could stay here. His wounds still throbbed hard and felt the need to sleep for a year but he was happy and content, for now.

Travelling through the night, dawn had bathed the now less harsh looking landscape in golden light as the knoll appeared in the distance.

Now the laughter and jovially had ceased and everyone looked pensive, riding back in single file once more, Ben could not see Mansours face but knew this man was vexed. He always thought he carried a lot of weight on his shoulders but this warrior, wise man and self appointed envoy among his people in front of him, carried a mountain. Clearly the man did not desire the shackles of leadership, fame or even fortune, only for this realm to prosper, yet this notion was going to get him killed.

The knoll itself was quite grassy with the odd boulder sticking out from it like a speared giant. As they reached the top there was a tremendous bustle around the camp. Neighing mounts and grunting big humped beasts with grand leather saddles were being taken away by tribesmen to be watered, fed and cared for; their owners lead to a cavernous bright yellow tent for much the same reason.

There were also many dark brown tents like Aamir's strewn around the large camp, the atmosphere, seemed very respectful and friendly, with many older tribesmen who Ben took to be the leaders, embraced each other warmly. Ben did not see it at first but next to the bright yellow tent was a tall narrow brown one without sides. On a solid timber table in the middle was what appeared like a large strange timepiece that looked completely out of place in a camp site of any kind. A tall gangly figure strode up to them and gave a small nod of his head to the men.

"Greetings, Muqrin the Overpowerer welcomes you all and bestows his famous hospitality to you as honoured guests".

"Does that mean that he wants to cut us in two" Usk whispered behind Ben's back.

"My name is Farouk, these men will look after your beasts as though as they were their own". He spoke to all four men but stared at Mansour the whole time.

"I respectfully ask if you two could follow this man" he gestured his open hand to a warrior standing next to him.

"He will take you to one of your officers sitting by the fires, please, eat and drink as you wish".

"Thank you" replied sergeant Usk politely as he marched towards the warrior.

Ben went with him but said "Good luck" clearly as he walked past Mansour.

He felt uneasy leaving Mansour with what awaited him but then swiftly remembered the man could fare for himself and was now in his element. "It is I who should be watching out" he said out loud". "Any idea which officer they would send out here?" he asked Usk who was clearly thinking the same thing.

"Well, look what the cat dragged in" came an excited but very familiar voice.

Ben stood back as a figure rushed on, only to reconise Lieutenant Kingswood as he snatched Bens's hand in his own and slapped his shoulder with the other.

"You look good for a slain man, sergeant", he still held the hand tightly and his eyes inspected the soldier closely with concern.

"You are wounded".

"I would gleefully settle for being alive at the moment".

Task swaggered into view and cleared his throat loudly.

"Sergeant Usk".

"Great sergeant Task", replied Usk as he snapped to attention.

The men from Mimas both gave an embarrassed cough and Ben snapped to attention as he saluted, Kingswood glanced around to see if anyone had noticed his un-officer like conduct.

"Lieutenant Pindar?", the Great sergeant asked hopefully as he glanced around the camp. Usk shook his head solemnly. "We all clearly have much to talk about" said Task deeply as he looked down at his boots, "this way, get a good meal down the both of you". They sat in front of one, of several camp fires and talked quietly about everything that had happened.

The men eat well and exchanged tales, Task was visibly rocked by the loss of Lieutenant Pindar. "He was by far the best of the young officers, he will be missed greatly by Diore, did his killer escape?".

"Mansour dealt with that" Usk said firmly with a wide smile.

At that moment the Tribal leaders left the tent and a very vexed looking Mansour walked briskly over to the soldiers.

"It is as I feared; Muqrin wants to become Emir of Io. Most of the other leaders do not wish it, so I had to defy his authority.

"He challenged you a contest with the sword?", asked Task fearing the worse.

Mansour nodded as the guardsman sensed that something was awry.

"You still do not believe you can defeat him?" he whispered glancing around the camp".

"It is not only that-".

At that moment Murqrin and Farouk calmly strode out from the tent.

"It is agreed then Mansour?, The contest will be at mid morning tomorrow in the ring of stones, by the ancient ways set out by the challenger".

The soldiers exchanged glances of befuddlement, even Task looked unsure.

"That means we fight to the death and the challenger's right hand can lay down his own challenge" explained

Murqin loudly, his mighty voice made the whole camp fall silent.

Farouk stepped forward as he spoke slowly, "I challenge you sergeant Hawks, with your champion of the Underworld sword".

"He cannot fight, look at the state of him, he is wounded", protested Kingswood passionately.

"You are the guest here of Muqrin the Overpowerer, Emissary, you will remain silent over tribal matters" Farouk warned dangerously.

"Can you not see in his face what this man has been through?, his wounds?" Kingswood carried on. He then took a huge breath. "We are both brethren from Mimas, if our lands are to forge an accord, then you must respect our honour as well. I wish to be this mans champion and fight as the right hand of Mansour.

"I will not let-".

"Silence Hawks, there is more at stake than your honour here" snapped the officer as his eyes kept on his host.

Muqrin raised his hand for complete silence and smiled broadly.

"For an Emissary your courage matches your wisdom, we do not seek challenges with the wounded in these lands but a challenge must still be fulfilled. I, - regretfully grant your wish, Emissary".

Time passed slowly but Ben was still furious he kept making excuses so he could avoid speaking to Lieutenant Kingswood. Eventually after volunteering to watch the Gold river for movements, he was by himself for a while until Mansour came by.

"You are a masterful warrior, you would be one of the finest swords in Mimas" he said swiftly to get it of his chest.

"Alas, we are not in Mimas", Mansour looked over at the clear blue waters of the great river and beyond. "I always liked Diore but have never travelled to Jovia".

"You have not missed much, you do not believe you can vanquish him?".

"I train hard, my skill with the sword is renowned in this part of Io", he then glanced back at the camp.

"Muqrin has fought many excellent warriors, yet I have been told he wears them all down and then despatches them. It is said he practises like a demonic soul day and night, it is his right hand, Farouk, who sees the running of the tribe and the lands.

The next morning the camp was again bustling but the air was thick with unease, Ben noticed it the moment he walked around the camp. His body was aching and he felt sluggish, as soon as Kingswood was awake he told him so and the two talked together about tactics and different styles of fighting they had witnessed since they arrived in these lands.

When the time came, he escorted the officer to a cleared flat strip of land to one side of the knoll. Two large circles of bright white stones were already laid out, a chirping bird flew softly overhead, Ben could not believe this idyllic scene would be a place of violence and death.

Mansour appeared at the same time, his hairy bare chest was glistening with sweat and the taut muscles flexed every time he moved. He wore a black sash around his waist, over his white baggy trousers and handed one over to Kingswood who wore the same garments.

Suddenly a commotion made all the men turn round as a heavy carriage was steered onto the top of the knoll by four dark grey draught horses. Ben had never seen anything like it before. As long as two normal carriages, it had a flat roof and was enclosed in thick timber with plates of metal riveted along the sides. The open hatches were quite narrow and even where the driver sat, the sides were covered by plate metal.

A massive, thick wooden strongbox was sat behind the carriage chained on stout metal brackets.

Eleven soldiers in dark grey uniform accompanied the carriage, Ben could see that one was plainly an officer but it was obvious the short bearded man riding next to him in a rich silk tunic had never fought anyone in his life. They drove past the stone circles and the man did not even seem to care who could hear him.

"Look at them!, pipe carving locals, really have no clue, do they?, barbarians, all of them" he muttered as he passed. They stopped close to the yellow tent and the bearded man and the officer dismounted and exchanged pleasantries with Muqrin.

"Charonese soldiers?, this is beginning to stink!" Kingswood mumbled.

"Beginning to make sense is what it is", snarled Task, his dark brown eyes appeared to darken as he saw the soldiers.

Muqrin allowed a bare chest Farouk to remove his flowing white cloak and head scarf to reveal a terrifyingly hardened body that could only be made with death in mind.

Aamir said something that made Mansour chuckle slightly only to see bemused faces on the other men.

"Aamir says he looks sloppy and fat", he explained, still smiling.

"At least that Farouk does not appear the same" said Ben trying to put his officer at ease.

"He is the only man Muqrin practices with" said Mansour, he was no longer smiling.

Muqrin the Overpowerer and his right hand walked slowly towards the stone circles as the grey uniform soldiers dismounted and all but one marched to join their officer overlooking the rings.

CHAPTER TEN

TIME WAITS FOR NO MAN

S tanding at the edge of their circle, far apart, Muqrin and Mansour stood upright facing each other, neither blinking or moving. In the other circle Ben could see Kingswood was ready but Farouk was kneeling on the ground, not in prayer but rested his right hand on the hilt of the sword, as the point balanced on the grassy surface.

The eldest of the tribal leaders, a withered but serene man, twice clanged a brass gong hanging from it's stand with a beater. The dull sound reverberated across the now silent camp, on the third, the fighters stepped forwards to battle.

Murqrin charged ahead and Mansour did the same, both raised their swords behind them and both blades flashed forwards to strike. Murqrin parried a blow to his throat only for a second to cut his thigh. He countered with a roar only to miss his target by a fair distance as Mansour turned on his heels and attacked again.

In the other circle the fighters were still carefully circling each other, trying to find out something about the other. Kingswood thought he had seen something and lunged forward to the head and then swiftly brought the thrust to the body as Farouk stepped outwards, glancing the blade to one side and then span around and carved his downwards, the startled officer sprang backwards and they circled around once more.

With one contest deciding if a war will take place and the other, the fate of a man who he admired and cared for, defending his honour, Ben was torn between whom he wanted to be watch, his eyes flashed between the circles as the spectators watched in calm respect.

"Have you seen that clock over there, never seen one like that before" stated Usk with interest.

"What?".

"That clock displayed over there under the tent. Metal base plate, sprouting four polished wooden legs with lavish brass clock face fixed between them, never seen anything like that, even at the palace".

Muqrin had missed once more with a deadly blow and Mansour darted in like a snake to sink his blade into his adversary's massive shoulder, then dashed away.

"Aamir said the Charonese gave it to Muqrin as a gift of friendship and he always keeps it close, he likes the prestige of such a modern contraption, it appeals to his vanity as a ruler.".

The guardsman snapped away from the contests and glowered at his fellow sergeant unable to believe what was being said.

"What are talking about??, it is just a bloody clock!", he glanced back to view the Overpowerer who was panting heavily, strike clear air again.

"Mansour's has him, he has...".

The words stuck in his throat as his ally darted in once more, only for Muqrin to drop his knees slightly and power forwards, smashing his bleeding shoulder into his opponents chest, knocking him cleanly off his feet and sending flying backwards.

Landing heavily on his back, the smaller man threw his legs up in the air and rolled over and pushed himself to his feet as a gleaming engraved blade flew over his head.

Muqrin the Overpowerer clearly liked to live up to his name, he brought his blade down time and time again with such brutal raw power that Mansour barely managed to hold his sword in his grasp as he blocked the devastating blows over his head. The spectators groaned as the brave warrior was forced down to one knee and then dive for his life to one side. The blow was so heavy, his owner had to dislodged his curved blade deep from the soil as he turned on his sworn enemy with fury. Springing to his feet he was beaten down for the second time, this time on his knees, though the etched blade still sliced his sword arm. He gritted his teeth to avoid crying out in pain and raised his head to see Muqrin standing over him. He spoke in a tongue that Ben recognised.

"Well, you came, you tried", his crimson blade rose up.

"Mansour cried out in sheer desperation as he leapt forward feet first, landing viciously on the knee of Muqrin as he did so. The big man crumpled slightly as the Lion faced him as his blade swished passed his foes belly.

As he doubled over, the conquer of the Underworld still held his infamous sword as the last attack came down, blood flowed freely from the gaping wound from his neck and chest. The man crashed down on his side, he struggled to push himself up, his huge body trembling uncontrollably, then fell again, this time staying down.

Kingswood and Farouk were still grimly fighting, their blades flashed through the air, the sight was dazzling. Both were bleeding from arm and torso wounds, as something made Farouk step backwards from the battle. He cried in anguish as he glanced at his fallen Master and then back at the officer in front of him.

His eyes burned with hate, then soften as he sighed with the heaviest of hearts, as he lowered his sword.

"You were a – worthy opponent but-now it no longer matters. He still needs me, I must go to him, that was always my only place".

Kingswood's eyes widened in horror as he understood the words too late.

"NO, wait, not like this!".

Farouk had already clumsily attacked and the Lieutenant instinctively parried and thrust in one motion. Piercing his heart, the sabre was still in his chest as Farouk collapsed into Kingswood's arms.

Mansour knelt down next to his foe, gasping for breath. With immense effort, Muqrin barely managed to lift his head from the grass to speak.

"You fought well, with skill and bravery, I die with honour" he wheezed.

"I had to, your name as the greatest warrior, will always live on in this desert".

This seem to satisfy him as he tried to smile but coughed heavily instead. His face was now twisted in pain and concern.

"You realise I did it for the people, other – lands will never leave us alone." He turned over painfully to view Leon.

"Those pale vultures over there, -are all the same, always they – value greed over – honour. I admit I was wrong – but can you ever trust them?". His body shuddered and his head rested on the grass, his eyes stayed open as he gazed over his beloved desert one last time.

"I trust two of them" Mansour said gently, staring at the prone figure. "That will have to do to begin with,- but I will always protect our lands".

He glanced over to a panting, bloodied Kingswood who was respectfully standing on the edge of the stone circle.

"Yes, you can come in now and well fought Lieutenant Kingswood!".

The officer grinned and walked unsteadily over, he was about to say something when a cry of warning came from one of the warriors guarding the tribal leaders.

Several musket shots rang out as bedlam engulfed the camp. Sensing something to his right, Kingswood dived to push Mansour down, as a musket ball struck him in the back, as another caught the Lion in his left leg. The fortified carriage trundled off as a petrified Leon was shoved into the cabin by Lieutenant Otto yelling orders to his men. A firm hand landed on his shoulder and span him around, as an enraged Task smashed a right cross on his chin. The groggy officer fell on his chest but still managed to tap one of Task's boots as he passed him, sending him sprawling across the grass. Task drew his sword as both men sprang to their feet and eyed one another carefully. Task lunged at the man but only made two strides as a musket ball flew through his left shoulder.

Incensed by the cowardly attack on his Lieutenant, Ben hurled himself into the affray by snatching the reins of a mount of a passing Charonese soldier. Yanking them down hard and screaming at the top of his voice, the beast panicked and unseated his master.

Kicking wildly with the hind legs, he trampled the unfortunate man underfoot as Ben revealed his new blade, wishing to draw it for the first time in anger.

More shots rang out and he could see the determined Great sergeant get right up and run through the nearest soldier whose bad timing cost him dearly.

Ben was about to assist him, when a mount with the Charonese officer nearly bowled him over. Seeking revenge, he glanced around and scythed a rider down from his mount in one deft blow and slowly hauled himself up by the reins. His wounds were searing in agony but wanted none of these murderers to escape. As he rode away he could see the handful of warriors guarding the camp, were finishing off the soldiers with relish as others rushed around to see to the wounded.

Every time a hoof hit the ground he grimaced in pain but kept his eyes on his prey ahead of him.

Hurtling down the side of the knoll he could see the carriage was in the distance and the officer was catching up with it. He also knew that the carriage could not sail across the river so unless they took a long diversion to the border, he could still reach them.

Reach them perhaps, be his mind was now wandering about what he could actually do if he did. All the good work of the healer seemed to have come undone.

He could now hear someone shouting and painfully turned on his saddle to see Usk and Aamir chasing behind him but they were further back still. Still riding hard, his heart leapt to see the carriage had slowed down close to the river and a sail boat with men armed with muskets were waiting alert, for any danger.

At that moment pain and fatigue overcame the guardsman and he slipped from the saddle, striking the ground head first.

Two soldiers released the four horses as Lieutenant Otto whose chin was bruised badly by the task's blow, went to the strong box at the rear of the carriage. Leon was already there, laughing and pointing to the men in pursuit of them.

"Those fools cannot stop us now, they are hopeless as those pipe carving savages".

Otto was about to answer when both men froze as they heard a whirring noise from the box and a long familiar chime started to ring out.

"They removed the gold and replaced it with the clock?, not so hopeless now are they!!".

Leon quickly recovered his wits and sneered at the officer.

"It appears they have blocked something in the lock as well, a simple challenge, they will never get the better of me!. Get your men to the boat, I can get this opened and turn the timepiece off in my sleep!.

Otto rolled his eyes and ran around the side of the carriage, ordering his men to ready the boat to depart post haste, he gathered some of Leons bags and threw them into the vessel with little regard of damaging them. Looking out for signs of danger he then dashed back to see Leon just standing there, appearing bewildered as he examined something in his hands.

The clock chimed for the tenth time as the whirring sound started again.

"I could not clear all the lock, I removed something, it -looks like- a piece of -wooden pipe!".

Lieutenant Otto looked on dumb struck, his shoulders slumped as the inevitable dawned on him.

"Oh, - you arrogant, -little sh...".

The carriage disappeared in a gigantic dark cloud as the unnatural noise echoed against the hills.

Pieces of knife edged metal sliced through the air at speed, so close to the bank the barge did not stand a chance and the sail and musket men alike were shredded by the murderous shards.

Ben felt someone grab him and his eyes blinked wide opened as he reached for a knife, only to see Usk grinning in front of him. Feeling light headed he allowed the amicable sergeant and Aamir to help him up as he surveyed the devastation.

"How?".

"The clock" explained Usk softly as he cast his eyes over the guardsman to make sure he was all right.

"Like I said, even the palace had nothing so grand. We saw that bearded sly looking man tinker with it, so Aamir and I decided to have a look while every one's eyes were on the contests. As I inspected it, I smelt the gunpowder in the wooden legs. It was faint but my father worked with the great cannons and I helped clean them, I can smell it twenty paces away".

"You put the clock in the strong box?".

"Aamir's idea, the gold is still at the camp".

Ben shook both their hands vigorously and feeling embarrassed, stared at Usk like they had never met before.

"I misjudged you, which was not your fault, I have learnt not to trust anyone except Lieutenant Kingswood."

"It appears to me that there are now at least three more you can trust. Let me began again, my name is Marc".

The men giggled as Aamir slapped the guardsman playfully on his shoulder.

"Marc, Aamir, my name is Ben", as he gazed at the remains of the carriage his mood darken, burning debris had blown in all directions and no trace of the officer or the strange bearded man could be seen.

"You have avenged the death of the best man I have ever met".

"Avenged??, your officer was still moving well and speaking when we left the camp".

Ben stared at the men in turn, unable to believe the words.

"Come, let us leave this place, go to your friend", continued Aamir as he helped the guardsman onto his saddle.

Eager to reach the camp but unsure if he could cope with more misery if Kingswood was too wounded to save, his head rocked with emotions.

As they arrived, Mansour limped from the bright yellow tent towards them. His white cloak had patches of blood all over it but his face was a mask of relief and glee.

"Our healer has taken out the musket ball from the Lieutenant, he is weak and has loss much blood but if he lives to the morning, he should heal well".

Ben hugged the man with delight, then stepped sheepishly back, remembering he did not hug people.

"That is better news than I expected" he murmured staring at the tent.

"Did those cowardly devils escape?".

"No, nor did they have a honourable death, it was quite barbaric" said Aamir with a half smile.

The next day Ben woke up outside the entrance to the yellow tent, a big fleece had been draped over him. As he struggled to his feet, he cringed in pain. His whole body was stiff and he realised his wounds had been bleeding again. He cleaned himself up with some warm water and redressed his wounds as he wandered back to his resting place and waited for news. The camp was peaceful and signs of any battle had long since been cleared away. A slight sound made him painfully spin around to see Mansour wearing a great smile.

"Lieutenant Kingswood is strong and has rested well. He cannot travel for a few days but he had good fortune".

"Officers always have!", exclaimed the guardsman as he gripped his ally's hand and shook it.

"Perhaps you can see him this afternoon, he needs to sleep".

"He shall have it, you and the healer have my eternal thanks. The camp seems, - less busy?".

Mansour shrugged his shoulders.

"The tribal leaders left last night after another gathering. At my request they have sworn to maintain a safe passage for all merchants through their lands, as before."

"Diore and Minmas will be relieved about that" Ben said gratefully.

"They are still deeply suspicious" his friend warned.

"They know that the men from Charon tried to provoke trouble".

"By trouble, you mean they tried to spark a war that would have cost thousands of lives and cripple the wealth of Diore and Minmas".

"Your words bring comfort when times are hard but you will never be a true Emissary, Ben", Mansour laughed heartily.

"I am not good with people, I told Lieutenant Kingswood the same thing".

"Ben, - the tribal leaders left, talking about the courageous officer who took his wounded sergeants place in the contest. That meant more than a hundred silky words. They were also incensed about the ambush and what went on in the Underworld, it is not their way. They will watch and listen for the actions of your people in the future. The two men were about to depart when the guardsman remembered something. "By the way, that move you did near the end of the contest?".

"The pounce?, the fox often pounces on the scorpion in the desert, to avoid getting stung badly.

"It is very effective, how many time have you tried it?".

"First time, I had tried everything else!, my strength was no more, I had nothing else to lose!!".

Later that afternoon, Ben was nervously kneeling over the Lieutenant. "Any more pale you would be a ghost".

The officer still had his eyes shut. "you really are a poor comfort to a wounded man, you know that?".

"Nether the less, you should not have risked your life for me Sir", his voice began to waver slightly. "I know Great sergeant Task was not impressed".

"Great sergeant Task can leap from the roof of the Citadel for all I care" whispered Kingswood weakly. "You risked your life to let us escape. Mansour told me how hard you fought in the Underworld and how you helped to free the others".

"Well, I had nothing else to do at the time!". Kingswood laughed out loud until he started to cough badly and wince in pain.

"He also told me you went after the men behind all this by yourself".

"I had help in the end, in fact Marc and Aamir did my work for me!".

"Still, you were foolish there, I have come to find you irreplaceable, you know that do you not?".

"I am sure Captain Nicolus could find you another good sergeant" he offered glancing at the carpet.

"Doubtful, and certainly not a better friend.

"Sir, - did you say..".

"Yes I did, anyway moving forward!. I have sent task off with two pieces of parchment that Mansour wrote down for me.

One is for the Princess, - to explain the situation here. The other is for Captain Nicolus, who I have respectfully requested that you are to be promoted to the rank of Great sergeant. I need you to have more authority, so you can assist me better in Diore".

Ben's eyes were wide open in surprise. "I am speechless" he spluttered".

"Well, there had to be a first time", Kingswood coughed again as he tried to talk in a serious tone. "You can be the one to inform Task, I am not that brave!".

Then Ben had a thought, "Sir, do you think Captain Nicolus will approve such a request?".

"Oh, I think so, saving the wealthy trading quarter of Almanthea does help to court friends!".

THE END

Also by Kevin Harris from
the Tales of Almanthea.

The Order Of Nemesis

Lightning Source UK Ltd.
Milton Keynes UK
UKHW040713090123
415051UK00002B/277

9 781958 381601